THE MAESTRO'S MAKER

RHONDA LEIGH JONES

ra❤enous
romance™

RS
RED SILK
EDITIONS

First published in paperback in 2010 by
Red Silk Editions
500 Third Street, Suite 230
San Francisco, CA 94107

First published as an e-book in 2009 by
Ravenous Romance
100 Cummings Center
Suite 123A
Beverly, MA 01915
www.ravenousromance.com

Copyright © 2009 by Rhonda Leigh Jones

All rights reserved. No part of this publication may be reproduced or transmitted in any form or by any means, electronic or mechanical, including photocopying, recording, or by any information storage and retrieval system, without permission in writing from Red Wheel/Weiser, LLC. Reviewers may quote brief passages.

ISBN: 978-1-59003-210-7

Cover design by April Martinez
Cover photograph © Literary Partners Group, Inc.
Printed in Canada

TCP

10 9 8 7 6 5 4 3 2 1

The paper used in this publication meets the minimum requirements of the American National Standard for Information Sciences—Permanence of Paper for Printed Library Materials Z39.48-1992 (R1997).

Chapter One

I WAS already a vampire the first time I met Claudio du Fresne—my love, my savior, my tormentor. He was a prisoner in the hold of the pirate ship captained by the albino Gunnar, who had been alive more centuries than even he could count. Gunnar was the one who had made me what I was nearly a year before. He was the cruelest man I had ever met.

It was August of 1788.

My job was feeding and watering the prisoners and changing their chamber pots. Gunnar reasoned that as a girl, I needed something to take care of. Besides: It was safer for me, as a vampire to interact with the prisoners than it would be for Gunnar's own men. Many of them were only wild young boys, too stupid to avoid being hurt by the desperate men waiting to become food for vampires.

On the night I met Claudio—then called le Compte Louis Claude-Michel du Fresne of Paris—Gunnar and his Cockney went with me to see the new prisoners. It was

Gunnar's ritual. The Cockney was most often the man in charge of procuring new prisoners, and he liked to show off what he caught. Today, he had a violin with him, which he had stolen from Claude-Michel.

Gunnar simply enjoyed striking fear into the hearts of new arrivals.

"God help us," someone whispered when the Cockney opened the door. The prisoners recoiled from the light of his lantern.

"My English friend, if I were not chained, I'd tear out your heart," Claude-Michel said.

The Cockney had led the party to capture Claude-Michel, his friend François Villaforte, and his young servant, Jean. He sneered, then spat on the floor and pointed at Claude-Michel with the violin. "Brave talk from a man who knows he'll never get the chance."

"Unchain me and find out," Claude-Michel said.

I had to step around Gunnar to see the prisoner. Hearing his French accent—I, too, was French—I looked immediately at Claude-Michel, ragged and noble in spite of his chains. He held his head in such a haughty way I had to admire him. He tried to smile at me. My heart broke.

I was sure Claude-Michel was the most handsome man I had ever seen. He was 43, but time had hardly touched him. His mischievous black eyes and full, shapely lips were complemented by a strong jaw line and large nose. His hair hung loose about his shoulders and threatened to curl on the ends. His blouse was loose and torn, revealing the hair on his chest. Even then, I wanted to see more.

I was a young woman of 18 then, older than many of the boys on that ship but young enough to dream of being saved from my predicament. Many men called my long, dark hair and large eyes beautiful; but I did not feel beautiful that evening. Gunnar had become angry that afternoon and broken open my lip. It had already begun to heal but was still visible, even in this light.

Claude-Michel did not seem to notice. "There was a time, *Mademoiselle*, when I would have given you a gallant bow and…"

Gunnar narrowed his pale eyes at Claude-Michel and smiled. "This one is much better than the others, Johnny," he said to the Cockney. "I may have to have him first."

The Cockney laughed: a sickening, sniveling sound. He was a gaunt, stringy boy baked by the sun; with limp hair so greasy it was brown instead of yellow. Most of his teeth were already rotten. Even more than the others, he smelled of the slow decay of mortality. "I told you we'd find something good, Captain," he said. The Cockney had led the band that had killed my family and captured me for Gunnar. I promised myself long ago I would kill him at my first opportunity.

"You will wind up with something you did not bargain for," Claude-Michel said, wrapping his hands around the links of his chains and pulling hard. "Unchain me. Have you any idea who I am?"

Gunnar took the lantern from the Cockney and approached Claude-Michel slowly, studying him with the unflinching intensity of a mountain. He was a large man, towering a full head over the others. He wore a brown fur vest that revealed well-muscled arms. His hair, a straight shock of white, reached to his chest, but was cut short on the very top. His skin was as white as the long bone earring dangling from his right ear.

Claude-Michel's eyes grew wide. "Albino," he hissed.

"No," Gunnar said conversationally, then stood. "I don't know who you are. But an interesting thing happens when you live to be as old as I have. You cease to care what people call themselves, what part they choose to play. The masks rot as soon as they die." Gunnar nodded slowly, narrowing his eyes and lowering his voice. "Oh, their descendants may keep up the ruse for a time. Mine did. But in the end it's just ashes and made-up stories to make the living feel better about their own dance with death."

Gunnar returned to me and fondled my breast with his back to the prisoners. I shuddered. He smiled at me while speaking to Claude-Michel. "Tell me," he said, "what role you played in life so that I may know what to pretend after your death."

"I am le Compte Louis Claude-Michel du Fresne, a noble at the court in Versailles, and owner of Du Fresne Shipping. You may be acquainted with my vessels."

Gunnar seemed to think for a moment, then shook his head. "No. Can't say that I am. But a count," he said, turning back to Claude-Michel. "Now that's a prize. I'll eat well for a while at least. It's so difficult to find a good meal at sea these days."

Claude-Michel pressed against the wall, eyeing him warily. "What are you—cannibal?"

Gunnar blinked and shifted his jaw sideways with a deliberate smile. "Before you are lost to that land from whence no man returns, why don't we enjoy a little entertainment?" He turned briefly to the Cockney. "Return the man's violin."

Grinning ridiculously, the Cockney sauntered over with the instrument. Claude-Michel sprang forward and grabbed him around the throat. "You idiot," Gunnar muttered and stepped forth to pull the Cockney from Claude-Michel's grasp and rip the violin and bow from his hand. These, he thrust at Claude-Michel. The two men locked eyes as Claude-Michel snatched the instrument away. He kept his mouth closed, breathing heavily through his nostrils.

"You will do us the honor of playing it," Gunnar said.

"Please, *Monsieur*," I said, surprising myself.

He looked at me, as though he had forgotten I was there, then returned his gaze to Gunnar. "For the lady, of course," Claude-Michel said, and began to play a haunting melody I had never heard. His chains rattled as he moved. He gave Gunnar a deadly glare, then tore his gaze from him and looked at me instead.

I was taken away. For a few moments, I forgot I was on that ship, and I loved him for that. He could have claimed me then as his and I would not have resisted.

When Claude-Michel finished, he tore the violin from his chin and stood swaying, still weak from the poison that had been used to subdue him. His hands trembled. He bowed. "What is your name, *Mademoiselle*?"

I glanced at Gunnar before answering. I felt as though I could barely speak, and was filled with such a terrible sadness that this man was being destroyed. "Chloe," I said.

"Chloe," he repeated. "Very nice."

Gunnar stepped in front of me. "And I am Gunnar. That was impressive, for an amateur. Gypsies. Why not something a little more modern?" he asked, reaching out his hand for the violin. Claude-Michel looked surprised. Gunnar nodded, once. I could see the spark of curiosity in Claude-Michel's dark eyes just before he handed him the instrument.

In Gunnar's hands, the Gypsy melody became organic, writhing around the room like a newly awakened creature dancing with spooky precision. I had never heard him play before. "How's your Austrian?" Gunnar asked, letting the melody fade into "Claire de Lune." This, he ended abruptly, making the violin screech. "Name anything. I can play it. Hum something and I will remember it a thousand years from now."

"You're mad," Claude-Michel whispered.

"Actually, I'm hungry," Gunnar said, moving to the shadowy corner across the room, where the line of prisoners began. Those on the far end whimpered and pressed against the wall as though plagued by visions of demons.

"*Monsieur,*" said the servant Jean, pressing against the wall, his eyes crazed with fear. Gunnar turned to him.

"Well. He speaks," Gunnar said, his voice slithering out like snakes. "And such a pretty one." He bored his gaze into the boy until Jean lowered his head, causing Gunnar to give a quiet chuckle and address Claude-Michel as he continued his slow walk along the row of men. "Oh, you three are safe for now. The poison in your system tastes terrible. You may be here an entire month before I decide to start the process of draining you, drop by drop. Until there's just a husk of the man you were." He stopped, and looked down at the man in the far corner. "It's your turn, Father."

The man shook his head. "No," he begged. "Please. No."

"What manner of man *are* you?" Claude-Michel asked.

"Yes," Gunnar whispered to the prisoner. "I, too, was a priest in my time, in the way of my people." Turning back to Claude-Michel, he continued. "And a great warrior. But that was eons ago. Since then I have been many things: prisoner, monster, farmer of souls." And here he smiled. "A god. At the moment, though, I'm captain of this ship." He turned to the cringing man. "Let's have a little communion, shall we, Father?"

The man's eyes widened. "Please..."

Gunnar looked at the violin and bow he held. "You won't miss this one very much. I hear Stradivarius is what people want now." He crumbled the instrument and bow in his hands like paper and spilled the pieces on the ground. My mouth opened in shock. I could see the sickness in Claude-Michel's face as he watched. The moment of peace had been an illusion. Only that hold was real. That ship. That stench.

"Gunnar!" I cried. "How could you do this?"

He narrowed his eyes at me. "One more word from you and I'll leave you in the first village I find. We'll see if all the old stories are true, of how they drive stakes through the hearts of those like you."

The threat made me go cold all over.

Claude-Michel struggled to his feet, and leaned his sweat-soaked body against the wall. Jean looked from him to me to Gunnar.

"Don't be so surprised," Gunnar said. "I have no need of an amateur violinist." Ignoring Claude-Michel's scowl, he turned to the cringing prisoner, removing the thin strap of leather from around his own neck. "Now Father, hold still." He unlocked the priest's shackles and made him stand. Then he motioned with his head toward Claude-Michel. "This man thinks I'm a monster," he said.

"Please, please don't," the priest said, and began to mumble something in Latin.

"Most of the people who find themselves in my hands start praying as though their souls depended upon it," he said. "I suppose we could say, then, that I am doing man a great service. Or God—bringing Him clean, newly confessed souls. Of course it doesn't happen all at once. It doesn't have to happen at all. Some choose to keep their meals as chattel. But I am so easily bored. I've always killed. Why stop now?"

He looked at Claude-Michel. "You have no idea what I'm talking about, do you?"

"The rantings of a madman," Claude-Michel snarled.

Gunnar's laugh, a loud, open-mouth roar, revealed his enormous canines. Claude-Michel furrowed his brow. Gunnar shook his head slowly. "No, my friend, you are not seeing things." He bared his fangs. "I am, indeed, vampire. And one day soon, you are going to see what it is like to be devoured. What delicious poetic irony. I'm sure you've been devouring people in your own way for years."

Claude-Michel swayed for a moment, as if on the edge of some terrible understanding. His legs buckled beneath him. The wall caught his weight as he slid back to the floor.

Gunnar smiled and turned away, put his hand in the priest's greasy hair, and forced his head to the side. Claude-Michel watched as Gunnar licked the young man's neck before fastening his mouth upon the flesh. Gunnar held the priest tight through the screams and struggles, and through their finish. I knew the young man's breathing would slow to mimic the rhythm of Gunnar's deep, hungry breaths. His frail fingers clutched his tormentor.

Claude-Michel crossed himself.

Gunnar raised his head, holding the priest against him. The young man's eyes were open, and blinked occasionally, but appeared not to see. "Not bad," Gunnar said. "But we should feed these people better. It would improve their taste."

"He was a man of God," Claude-Michel whispered.

"Was?" Gunnar replied. "He is yet. For a little while longer. And soon he'll collect his reward."

"What *are* you?" Jean asked.

Gunnar pushed the dazed priest at the Cockney, who nearly dropped him. The priest's dulled eyes tried to follow Gunnar as he sauntered over to Jean. Claude-Michel stiffened.

"What am I," Gunnar said, emphasizing his words with movements of his hand. His movements were not so delicate as those of Claude-Michel, but they were graceful. "I live off the blood of others, my dear boy. The mere sight of meat, which I once ripped raw from the bones of my enemies with my bare teeth, now turns my stomach. I must pierce living flesh and dine on the sweet juices beneath. I am a *vampire*," he nearly whispered, smiling. "You will see."

"Monster," Claude-Michel hissed.

"Probably," Gunnar said. "But what does it matter? I live, and I'll go on living. I'm afraid neither can be said about any of you. Come, Chloe." To the Cockney, he said, "Bring him."

The sound of my name startled me. I looked at Claude-Michel before turning to follow. *I will save him*, I thought. *Somehow, I will save him*.

Chapter Two

I WALKED among men without fear. I dressed like a boy in trousers and loose blouses, and tied back my hair with a thin strip of leather. It had been used to bind documents belonging to one of Gunnar's unfortunate meals, who were usually men caught off-guard or drunk in alleys and bars, or boys looking for a new life. These were desperate boys who thought going to sea would keep them from starving; boys in search of adventure; lonely boys who wanted nothing more than to belong somewhere. Those who couldn't prove themselves to Gunnar's satisfaction found themselves chained below, awaiting a slick, messy death.

My stomach rumbled at the thought of so much blood. I hadn't fed in days, and was beginning to feel the first pangs of a deep hunger that would grow quickly. I felt annoyed that my body would try to drive me inside on such a beautiful night. Even after most of a year, I was still amazed at the things I could see in what I had once called darkness. My eyes had learned to capture even the faintest bit of light, which revealed to me all the secrets and wonders that humans could never see—the tiny mouse cowering in a corner, the things that swam beneath the surface of the water, the faintest tic in a man's face.

Shadows had no power over me, nor did darkness or the venomous whispers through clenched teeth of cowardly men.

I had passed several of them after leaving Gunnar's cabin. Some sneered even while long-buried instincts swam up from the deep and pleaded with them to take flight; others cast down their eyes and pretended not to see me. All of them, afraid.

I wondered why I had ever found these men threatening. They were weathered and rough looking, yes, but very young. Bloodthirsty boys with ragged faces and knobby limbs, teeth brown or black or missing, breath fetid. The stench was always present, that poisonous mortality rising through bodies that begun to rot the day they were born. With eternity surging through my own veins, I was exquisitely aware of the slow decay of normal human flesh, and that made me feel vastly superior.

The Cockney with limp, yellow hair who had chased me through the woods 10 months before now sat in my favorite spot on an overturned barrel near the rail, smoking. Anger prickled down my spine. Fear of Gunnar was the only thing keeping me from ripping out the Cockney's throat, and he knew it.

I slowed my pace, planting one boot on the deck, waiting for the sound to register before planting another. The Cockney began to fidget. He took a long drag from his pipe and turned his tiny, vapid eyes on me. He had the look of a cowardly, feral dog. And, because of the change, I was several inches taller than I had been when Gunnar had first brought me on board more than three seasons earlier.

My eyes narrowed. I wondered if my hands would one day murder him on their own.

The Cockney looked away, as though sensing the thought. Every detail of his face—from week-old stubble along his jaw to an enflamed fly bite on the side of his neck—was as clear to me as it would be by daylight. I kept my eyes on him as I drew near the deck rail. Fear wafted from his skin as pungently as did the odor of unwashed flesh, and that made me smile.

When his hands began to shake, he stood and forced himself to keep his eyes on me as he passed by before retreating below. I wondered if he realized I could hear him mutter "Bitch," when he thought he was safely out of reach. He knew I could snap his neck without trying very hard, and that was all that mattered.

I leaned against the rail and , and refused to think about him any more, preferring instead to fix my mind on the water below, which told me secrets, showed me the sharks keeping pace with the ship in the dark wetness, the school of fish that darted ignorantly in their wake, keeping blissful company with predators. I shifted my gaze to the expanse of tiny waves and undulations between myself and the horizon. *If I could see eternity*, I thought, *it would look like that ocean, murky and infinite.*

I began to think about the man in Gunnar's cabin, whimpering for his life. His veins were a tangle of sweet tendrils, his pulse a tempting fruit ripe to bursting. There was no guilt for me in wanting his throat, since I discovered they didn't die when I fed. Gunnar killed them for pleasure. He had told me this when he first brought me on board. I assumed he was trying to scare me, but I was already ill from the bite. It hurt so badly: my body devouring itself from the inside out. When it rebuilt itself, I wanted to die. Then the hunger came, and nothing else was important. A new strength surged through my veins. I had been reborn.

Part of that strength, I now knew, was the hatred I felt for the men who had murdered my husband and children. It gave me such pleasure to see them slink away at my approach, to hear their hearts flutter like little rabbits in my presence.

And to dream of cutting off Gunnar's head and feeding it to the sharks.

When I arrived in the captain's quarters, where I lived with him, Gunnar was propped in his bed, reading a book with a peeling spine. Several of its pages were loose. It had to be held together with an old piece of leather like the one I wore in my hair. I had seen it many times, and thought the gold lettering on the cover was pretty, but could not read what it said.

Gunnar's room contained many books secured in cabinets, piled on the floor, and tossed aside without care. But Gunnar always knew where each one was. He was a shepherd of lost words. To me, they were mysterious, forbidden things.

"What is that book?" I asked, careful to avoid the puny, frightened creature cringing in the corner, his ankles and wrists raw from the metal cuffs. The priest's fear-crazed eyes followed my every movement.

"*Paradise Lost,*" Gunnar replied without looking up.

"Oh," I said. "What is it about?"

He turned the page. "Devils who were once angels but were cast into the pits of Hell by a vengeful god, like Hephaestus, falling forever among the ruins of earth, crippled and despised." Without warning he turned his white eyes on me. "Like us."

I caught my breath when he said that, but recovered quickly. "I have never been an angel, *Monsieur*. But I am nothing like you."

Gunnar shifted his jaw to the side the way he always did when considering what to do with me. He put aside the book and got to his feet. I think I felt, more than heard, the movement of the man in the corner. My fangs extended from my gums like cats' claws. I ran my tongue over them, grimacing when it came in contact with the points.

Vampires' fangs extend themselves for three reasons: hunger, sexual desire, and fear. I felt humiliated that my body would show such an obvious sign of alarm, so I shut my mouth tight and made myself concentrate on this tower of a man who stood too close to me, and who smelled like the dust of long-forgotten ruins. Gunnar's voice seemed monstrous and opaque like the ocean, which cradled foul, ancient creatures.

"You're not like me?" he asked.

My heart fluttered but I stood my ground, focusing on the shocks of white hair falling jagged over his massive chest and the tiny white bone dangling from his ear. I'd never had enough courage to ask who it had been.

"What was your last meal?" he continued. "Or should I say, who?"

I involuntarily looked where he looked, at the priest. He had explained in broken, terrified sentences that he was on his way to help the poor when he had been captured. Maybe God would have some mercy on our souls, he said that day. But he had been desperate. I knew most men didn't believe we had souls in the first place; that we were condemned to Hell simply for being what we were.

This man was young, on his first assignment alone. He felt he was too young to die. He had wandered too far from the carriage when it was time to relieve himself in the woods. Gunnar himself had been there, and had taken him swiftly, without a sound. Now he was cringing in the corner, naked. His ribs moved too quickly with his panting breaths. Even now his lip quivered.

"Please," he whispered, barely loudly enough for even a vampire to hear.

"Quiet," Gunnar said, "or I'll slit your throat tonight."

The priest linked his fingers and began to pray.

Gunnar smirked at me. "I haven't touched him, other than to bring him here. I got him for you, my darling little French milkmaid."

"That doesn't mean anything," I said quietly. "I'm not a—" I couldn't quite say it, because I was afraid I was becoming like him. I closed my mouth and bit my lips shut like I had done since I could remember. But now, the points of my teeth made me bleed. The blood tasted like pennies.

"A what?" Gunnar sneered. "You're not a what?"

"A murderer."

He laughed. It was a deep sound. He came closer and closer, but I curled my toes tightly inside my boots and did not move. His voice slithered out. "Not a murderer? Oh yes you are. In the eyes of the world, and that's all that matters. Perception is truth, my dear Chloe. If they get you, they'll try to hang you with the rest of us, for piracy on the open sea. Do you know what will happen then? When they discover they can't kill you by hanging you, they'll devise a thousand tortures to prove you're a witch. You'll be better off telling them you're a vampire right away."

"I'll tell them you forced me."

"They won't care. Don't you understand? There is no compassion in men's hearts for what they don't understand. I'm all you have in this world. Your only protector." He sneered down at me, and flipped a lock of my hair in his fingers. "Even with all your new strength, you're still just a girl. A scared little girl who can't take care of herself." He narrowed his eyes and lowered his voice until his words ran out in a smooth, liquid hiss. "Except to the world. To them, you're a monster, and they would love to rip you apart." He drew out the word "love," letting me see his tongue linger on his sharp teeth.

I tried not to, but I shuddered. I hated him for being so aware of my weaknesses. And I hated being so hungry.

"You had better eat," Gunnar said, turning from me.

I looked at the huddling form in the corner, but could not manage to work up an appetite. "I'm not hungry," I said.

Gunnar turned back to me then, taking my upper arms in his strong hands and nearly lifting me off my feet. He looked into my eyes, letting a lecherous smile stretch his lips, revealing his fangs to me. My fangs had grown as well, because he had startled me, and because of a desire I felt, but did not want.

"Then I will have you, my child," he said and began removing my clothes as the priest chanted in Latin from the corner.

Gunnar's body was like iron. He was as strong as he was old, strong even for a vampire. Being taken by him was like being caught in a storm. When he laid me, naked, back on the mattress, I thought of the beautiful Frenchman in the hold, and felt I should be making love with him instead of taken by Gunnar. At the last moment, I pushed at him and tried to squirm away. "No!" I shouted. "I don't want to! Get off of me! You're a monster!"

It was a lie and he knew it. I hated that his body did this to mine, hated the fact that I grew wet every time I thought about his hard, unyielding shaft penetrating me, the strength in his hips as he pounded into me with a force as ancient as the trees. I hated that he was beautiful and that the animal smell of him made me want to arch my back and growl deep in my throat, and that I wanted to beg him to fuck me. I never had, but my mind screamed it silently. My body always moved on its own under him.

Gunnar laughed deep in his throat. "Oh, Chloe," he said, shaking his head and sliding his fingers inside of me. "Foolish, young Chloe. Stop fighting, child."

The certainty and calm in his voice killed my will to fight. Breathing heavily, I submitted to his touches, and to the arousal he created in my body.

Gunnar opened his breeches and settled between my legs, pushing at me with his erection. My body did not want to let him in, but he was patient, working his penis against my folds, teasing me with a little smile on his face. He was perhaps the most patient man in the world, an ancient predator.

He made my body yield to him, slipping his engorged member into me bit by bit, making deep grunting noises, filling me up. "Ah, yes," he said with a smile when he was all the way in. "My Chloe."

I thought of the first time with him on the forest floor near my home, the day I was captured, the day I was changed. I had screamed when he showed me his fangs. He had placed his finger over my lips, working his hips against me in little movements. "Shh…" and this, for some reason, had calmed my mind.

"I am your lord and master," he had said that day, and pinned my wrists to the ground, taking me without mercy, and without regret.

I had never been fucked the way Gunnar had fucked me that first time, forcing my legs apart and grinding into me, slowly at first, filling me to the hilt with every single thrust. I hadn't wanted to respond, but my body couldn't resist.

Nothing had changed. I felt myself grow aroused against my will as Gunnar watched my face. He studied me while pulling the length of his erection out of me slowly, covered with juices that I did not want to give him. He smiled while sliding into me again, deeper, claiming me. Soon his thrusting became so forceful that I forgot how much I hated him, and just lay there gasping, as I did each time he took me. My insides were on fire. There was nothing I could do.

Except bide my time.

Chapter Three

CLAUDE-MICHEL'S SERVANT, Jean, was a girlish, pale-skinned boy with delicate features and honey-colored hair. When I brought them their meals the next evening, I found him looking at me, blinking in the light of my lantern. I smiled. "I hope you're going to be more talkative than he is," I said, nodding to a silent prisoner in the corner. "He's been like that since he was brought here."

"Why should we entertain you while we wait to be killed?" Jean spat. "I don't want your food!" It was not the way he normally behaved, but I didn't know that then. I did not know what to say.

"Jean!" Claude-Michel said. "Did I teach you these manners?"

The Frenchman's tone made me shiver. Even as a prisoner fated to die, he seemed strong and commanding. Jean and I turned to him, startled.

"I am sorry, *Monsieur*. Forgive me," Jean said and grew silent.

I felt I should say something. "Will he eat if you tell him?"

Claude-Michel nodded, once. "Unless he wants stripes across his beautiful back when your captain comes to his senses and releases us."

His spirit touched me, and saddened me as well. "I am sorry, *Monsieur*," I said quietly. "That will not happen. But he will perhaps amuse himself with that priest for a week or more."

"And after that?" Jean said in a softer tone than before. He looked up at me with such round, frightened eyes, I wanted to cry for him. "Will I be next?"

Jean noticed that Gunnar seemed to be working from the side of the room nearest him.

"Eat," I said. "Or you will be too weak to care." I wanted to reach out and comfort him with my touch, but didn't dare. It did not pay to become too attached to Gunnar's intended meals, and I already felt something for his master.

"No, *cher*," Claude-Michel told him. "Not if I have any influence here." When I looked up, he was staring at me so intently I had to look away.

I moved on to Claude-Michel's friend François, who stared straight ahead with fevered blue eyes. Gunnar's men used poison-tipped weaponry when they went out in search of prey, and there were usually no injuries. But these men had fought hard, and François had been cut badly in the arm. His blond hair was plastered to his face and neck with sweat. He could not eat, no matter how I tried to entice him, or what Claude-Michel threatened. When I touched his forehead, it felt as though his skin would scorch me. "I did not realize it was so bad," I said. François flailed his arm and babbled nonsense. He was already too far gone with infection to recover. If Gunnar found out, he would simply pitch him to the sharks.

I did not say any of this.

When I made my way to Claude-Michel, he was still looking at me. He tried to touch my face with his fingertips, but I flinched backward, remembering my lip. It was still just a little swollen.

"Cherie," Claude-Michel said softly. "Who has been treating such a lovely creature so terribly?"

"Gunnar is rarely a nice man," I said.

"How did you come to be with him?" Claude-Michel asked.

I did not want to answer. "I am sorry about your violin. Nothing is sacred to Gunnar—not God, not music. Not life. Nothing."

A dark, pained expression crossed Claude-Michel's face. "Yes. It was a lovely instrument." He gestured with his hand. "But it's nothing, a tool of seduction." In spite of his predicament, he smiled. "It worked, no?"

I lowered my eyes briefly. "I loved your playing. I have not heard music in a long time." I let myself get too close, and Claude-Michel struck out his hand to seize my wrist. I pulled out of his grasp easily. He raised his brows.

"Very strong," Claude-Michel said with a snicker. "You must have grown up on a farm."

"Yes," I said, realizing his words were not a compliment. "I worked very hard."

"But such delicate features."

"What can I say, *Monsieur*? Some of us are born lucky."

"Are you on the menu?"

The question startled me, and cut through my anger. I lowered my head. "No. Yes, I—He does what he wants with me, that is all."

Claude-Michel pressed on. "Then he has not lost the ability to appreciate a beautiful woman."

Something about the tone of his voice, the accusations there, made me fear I would burst into tears. "Please eat," I said, and got to my feet in one fluid movement before retreating without the lamp.

"Chloe," Claude-Michel began. "My friend is going to die soon if something isn't done."

"Then he dies soon, rather than later," I snapped, unable to keep my voice from quaking. "It doesn't matter. You're all going to die."

Claude-Michel pressed on. "This ...Gunnar of yours ... likes to kill. Oh, but I forget. He's a vampire."

I paused at the door, resigned to the conversation, aware that I would have to return for my lantern. "He says when a man is his age, he has experienced everything there is and knows how cheap life is. This is one of the only pleasures that still makes his heart pound, he says."

Claude-Michel smiled and gave me an expression of mock innocence that made me want to touch him. Afraid I would lose control and do just that, I hurried back into the room, reclaimed my lantern and hurried back to the door. His voice stopped me again. "Chloe, when a man is my age, one of his greatest pleasures is keeping a clean-shaven face."

"I cannot give you a blade," I said.

"But you could shave me yourself. I think I trust you not to cut my throat."

I turned and met his eyes. "But can I trust you not to cut mine?"

Claude-Michel lifted his wrists and again tried the innocent expression. "I am quite helpless, *Mademoiselle*. Between these chains and your charms, I have no powers left with which to defend myself. But I am a *compte*. I don't want to die looking like a vagabond."

"He will kill the priest soon," I said, because I didn't know what else to say.

Claude-Michel paused and cocked his head. "He likes to kill. Why does he not do the same to you?"

I narrowed my eyes at him, suspicious that he knew I was a vampire. I was careful with my words. "He does other things to me."

"He doesn't allow you to hear music," Claude-Michel said softly, compassionately. "That is very close to death."

I shook my head. "There are no musicians on the ship, except for you. These boys…they are useless for anything other than killing. And many of them cannot even manage that."

"I am no musician," Claude-Michel said. "All gentlemen know how to play, as all know how to make love. Some are simply better than others."

My mouth went dry. I knew he was keeping me there, making me want him on purpose so I would help him. I could feel myself sliding closer and closer to his trap. "Are you better than others, *Monsieur*?" I asked. He responded only with a slow blink and a smile. I cleared my throat. "I am sorry about your violin. I felt its death."

"I would play for you all of the time if we were free, my dear."

I nodded. "I know what you're trying to do."

"Yes. I am trying to get you to set us free. And yourself. You would come with us, of course. And I would show you the pleasures of making love, which are very much unlike what you feel when you are being used by some monster."

"I have to go," I said and hurried away, leaving them in the dark.

"He'll grow tired of you one day," Claude-Michel called after me. "What will you do then?"

I will not be here long enough to find out, I thought.

Chapter Four

LATER THAT night, I wandered aimlessly around Gunnar's quarters while he sprawled on top of his mattress, feeding with the young priest under him. I had not yet managed to work up an appetite and felt bored. As for the human suffering mere yards away, I had come to terms with Gunnar's sport long ago and willed myself to think of his human prey as animals.

If I could read, I told myself, *Gunnar's room would be endlessly fascinating.* There were cabinets of books and contraptions kept latched so they wouldn't spill in stormy weather, and stacks of other books on the floor and in Gunnar's chair. More books, and devices like an abacus and various types of compasses, littered the table. There were scrolls in the corners, and maps and sketches on the walls. The room was a testament to Gunnar's curiosity about the very people he used so carelessly.

When Gunnar finished, he raised his head and took a deep breath. "Magnificent!" he said. "The pious always taste so much better than the sinful hordes." The priest's head lolled. He tried to say something in Latin. Gunnar chuckled. "He's trying to exorcise my demons. How nice of him." He fingered the crucifix dangling from the young man's neck. He had ordered his men to leave it there. "With all of their advancements, they are still wearing talismans to ward off evil spirits." To the priest, he said, "Cease that chatter or I will rip off your scrotum with my bare hands. I am already bound for Hell."

I looked over my shoulder at him.

"Drink," Gunnar said to me. "You haven't dined in days."

My stomach rumbled, surprising me. My hunger had come and gone over the past few days, but now it sprang to life, violently, so I joined Gunnar on the bed.

I felt myself kneel on the mattress and reach toward the young priest's hot, seething flesh. Like a cornered rat, he tried to flail away from me, but Gunnar would not let him move. "Now, now, Father," he said.

I burrowed into the hollow beneath his jaw and penetrated the tender flesh of his throat to find that luscious, throbbing fruit just beneath the skin. But the fruit seemed overripe, and its smell sickened me. My fangs retreated. Feeling as though I might vomit, I clutched my belly. The priest babbled thank-yous at me. I wanted him to be quiet.

Gunnar furrowed his brow at me thoughtfully. "This is a queer time to become squeamish," he said, leaning in toward me and studying my face. "You've never agreed with my methods, but you've never turned down a meal."

"I don't feel well," I said.

He narrowed his eyes at me. "That is not a ruse you can work with me, Chloe. Vampires do not become ill," he said.

I sat up. The room spun. Keeping my head very still, I looked around wildly. "That is what you say. But now I see it's a lie," I said, while the priest shuddered beside me. "If this is immortality, you may take it back."

Gunnar took my jaw in his large hand and made me look at him, to study my face. "It cannot be," he muttered to himself. There was something approaching fascination in his voice.

A great pain surged through my gut and caused me to sweat all over. I thought about taking off my clothes, but did not want to be naked again in front of the priest. I had not felt anything like this since becoming a vampire. It was terrible. The sight of stray droplets of blood, which usually filled me with desire and hunger, nauseated me until I thought I would die, even though I was very hungry. If I hadn't felt so ill, I would have been scared to death.

Chapter Five

THE NEXT morning, I felt fine. I went about my day, reporting to Gunnar and making sure the men did their jobs. But my mind was on the prisoners in the hold. Gunnar retired early to his room to read, so I decided to feed them early.

They got gruel and stale bread—pretty good fare compared to what I was usually able to scrounge up for them. Claude-Michel didn't seem to think so, however. I sat near him, moving my lantern near so that he could see me in the darkness. Aside from that one source of light, everything in that room was black to mortal eyes. Rats roamed freely through the hold, often biting the prisoners. But rat-bite fever did nothing but sour the meal a little, so Gunnar did not care.

Claude-Michel glared at me. "I am not accustomed to eating with my hands. Do you think I could have a utensil?"

"Prisoners aren't allowed," I told him. "I am sorry."

He grunted and began to use his bread to bring the soupy gruel to his mouth. His chin had darkened with a layer of coarse hair. "My friend is dying," he said.

I looked at François. He appeared to be sleeping peacefully, but I knew he didn't have long. His arm was terribly inflamed, running with pus and other foul liquids. Next to him, Jean concentrated on his plate of food, ignoring me.

"Everyone who finds himself chained in this room is dying," I said. "But I haven't been as sorry about that as I am now, after meeting you. I wish I had known you before."

Claude-Michel looked at me then, chewing slowly. "How did you come to be with such a man?" he asked.

I hugged my knees to my chest like a child. "Last autumn, his men came and destroyed my home. Killed my family. They would have killed me, but Gunnar wanted me for himself. So here I am."

"You are a prisoner."

"Yes," I said quietly.

"You are French."

I nodded. "I am from the countryside. You were right. My husband was a farmer. Gunnar likes to insult me by calling me a milkmaid. But it isn't insulting. We were happy there." I felt myself blush. I was not educated, but I knew what men like him thought of women like me, no matter how I painted life in the countryside. Normally, I would never be interesting to him, but now, I realized, I was his symbol of hope, as he was mine.

"Tell me about your life," I said. "How do you come to be here?"

I did not think his face could darken more, but it did. "I killed a man in the street and had to leave France. He was a poor man, and the poor are rioting. They would have demanded my head. It is a very dangerous time for nobles there, especially in Paris."

"Killed a man?" I asked. It was not what I had expected to hear. "Why?"

"Because he killed my son, for no other reason than Gabriel was of noble birth. I was making arrangements for him to marry." The darkness in his face turned to sadness. He blinked his beautiful eyes and swallowed.

I leaned over and put my hand on his arm. "You grieve your child as I grieve my children," I said.

He looked at me, chewed slowly and swallowed, but did not move away from my touch. "My daughter also. She was fourteen. I went to my brother's house in Florence, to wait for François to bring my wife and daughter. But when he arrived..." Claude-Michel's words became ragged as he struggled not to sob. "When he arrived...he had only Jean with him. He said the crowds had learned of the murder and taken their vengeance upon my family."

His chin quivered. Then he took a breath. "Forgive me," he said, attempting to wave his passions away with his hand. "I loved them deeply. A man is nothing without his family."

As he told his story, my own eyes filled with tears. "What were their names?"

Claude-Michel looked into the middle distance, as though he could see their faces hovering in the air. "Angelique, my wife. She had the most beautiful red hair and green eyes. Our son, Gabriel, was more like me, with dark hair and a quick temper. We did not always see eye to eye. But he was defending me that day. That is why he was killed. Defending his father." He swallowed, then continued. "My daughter had soft blonde curls, the color of Jean's, and she was an angel. The most beautiful creature I have ever seen. Camille was her name.

"We were returning to Paris to find the bastards who killed them and make them pay when your—Gunnar's—men accosted us." He spat out Gunnar's name with all of the venom I felt. Then he looked at me again.

"I am so sorry, Claude-Michel," I whispered.

Over the next few days it became my habit to remain with them as they ate. In time, François was able to take enough food to keep himself alive, but gangrene had set in. The stench would have been horrible for a mortal man, and it took every bit of willpower I had to force myself to stay in that room.

Seeing Claude-Michel's eyes brighten when I came in made it worth the stench, and the danger of getting caught. On one particular evening, a mischievous light shone in Claude-Michel's black eyes. "Oh *Mademoiselle*," he said. "The things I would do with a woman like you. You would enjoy a firm hand, I think, as my Angelique did."

His words startled me and sent a jolt of arousal through my belly.

"What do you mean?" I asked, intrigued.

"Let me tell you of what happened the night I had to go to the whorehouse to find my son, on the very night we were to be at a palace gathering. He was to meet with the du Peliers, with whose lovely daughter I was trying to arrange a marriage. François was to take Angelique and Camille home, but of course, Angelique preferred to wait at the palace for me. I do not accept disobedience."

Gunnar didn't either, but hearing Claude-Michel say it caused me to shiver pleasantly. "What did you do?" I asked as innocently as I could.

"I took her across my knee and I spanked her, of course."

"Tell me," I said.

He tilted his head at me then, and lowered his lids enticingly. "As you wish," he said. "My Angelique's body was the color of cream. It was beautiful, even though we had been together for many years. Our son was twenty-two. So I ordered her to take off her gown, and I told her, 'You should never disobey me, Angelique, even in the smallest things.' I watched her shiver at my words. She said, 'Forgive me, *Monsieur*.' She called me this when she knew I was about to punish her. I will not lie," he said, smiling. "It excited me. I told her she was forgiven, of course."

I had never considered such a thing exciting, but now felt as though I was discovering sex for the first time. I wanted to hear more about how my beautiful countryman had punished his wife.

"I sat on the couch in my bedroom with her across my knee and laid my hand upon her perfect *derrière* while she waited. 'I hope the comtesse doesn't think this is a game,' I told her. 'While I may enjoy seeing you sprawled helplessly across my knee, I am anxious that you take this correction seriously. The very next time you fail to follow my orders, you will get more than my hand against your derrière. Do you understand?' And she said, 'Yes, *Monsieur*,' which excited me further.

"I shifted myself beneath her so she could feel me becoming excited. I was ready for her, but I enjoyed what I was doing very much. I knew I could take my time. When I began to spank her, she jumped, but was very good and did not cry out. I praised her. 'Very good,' I told her. 'It would not do for our children to rush in here and see their mother in such a compromising position, would it? To see you lying across their father's lap, while he spanks you as he would a little girl, perhaps as their equal, or someone beneath them.'"

"That's terrible," I said, more breathlessly than I intended.

Claude-Michel gave me his most innocent look. "I am a terrible man, *Mademoiselle*."

"Why do you call me that?" I asked. "I was a married woman."

"Because, to me, you are a girl in the prime of her beauty."

I lowered my eyes. "Thank you, *Monsieur*."

He took a moment to give me a look I would have found irresistible if circumstances had been different before resuming his story. "I taunted her mercilessly, striking her *derrière* harder. She began to make muffled cries against the cushion, but still she was very careful. She begged me to stop and swore she would never disobey me again, something she had sworn many times over the years. I caressed the pink flesh gently…" His voice trailed. Again, his eyes became distant. "It was the same on our wedding night. She had begged me to let her go; convinced her parents had delivered her into the hands of a madman. But I probed until uncovering the seeds of darkness in her, and nurtured them, until the mere threat of punishment had begun to make her wet. Afterward, of course, I took her to bed and made such love to her. I will never forget what she said to me when I asked if she had enjoyed it: 'Enjoy. What a strange word to describe how I feel about the things you do to me.'"

"It is…understandable," I said, barely able to get the words out. I wanted him badly. I had never wanted a man this badly in my life.

Claude-Michel dragged his hand across his jaw. The sound of flesh scraping against whiskers made my skin crawl. "This beard is appalling," he said. "I am not accustomed to it."

I nodded, reminded he would soon become hairy like a beast, no longer beautiful. He would lose weight and become gaunt. Only then would Gunnar begin to play with him.

"I am sorry, *Monsieur*," I said. "Please finish your dinner. I must go soon."

* * * *

When I returned to Gunnar's room, I tried again to feed, but the smell of blood made me twice as sick as before. I lay on the bed panting, not caring if Gunnar killed me on the spot. I felt so sick I wished he would.

But he did not kill me. He merely dragged the priest off the bed and chained him in the corner again, then returned and took my jaw in his hand, turning my head from side to side. He opened my eyelids to examine my pupils, and furrowed his brow. "Perhaps you really *are* going into phase. I thought perhaps you were sulking."

"Into phase...?" I said.

"Yes," he said, letting me go. "This is strange. It didn't happen to me for years. I was in phase when you came to me. It's why I spared your life. It's why I was able to turn you into the magnificent creature you are now."

Patches of darkness swam at the edges of my vision. "Why you were...? What does it mean? What's happening to me?"

"You will continue to refuse food for a time," he said, his voice almost gentle. "I have always suspected that it is to prevent too many vampires being made."

I took several deep breaths, trying to understand his words and keep myself from vomiting at the same time.

"If you feed during this time...if you force yourself to bite another, your bite will cause him to become a vampire."

"I thought—" I put my hand to my forehead.

"You thought what, child?"

I fought to keep my eyes open, to keep from heaving. "I thought you knew some sort of magic."

He gave me a condescending smile. "No. There is no magic. Science, yes, but no magic."

I closed my eyes, vaguely relieved I was not dying. Gunnar picked me up and placed me into the bed. I groaned and begged him to leave me alone, told him he was killing me. He soon settled down to read, but I kept worrying the idea of being in phase. It meant something to me, something important. It was hard to think through the nausea and pain in my gut. But finally, I got it. My heart pounded furiously. This was it, the thing I had been waiting for. I knew this was how I could save the handsome Frenchman and myself. If I couldn't find a savior to take me home, I could make one. And what better champion than my own countryman?

The plan I finally devised the following morning, when I felt better, involved stealing Gunnar's razor.

Chapter Six

IT WOULD be difficult to get near Claude-Michel. I considered seducing him, but I was no seductress. Kissing his neck so I could bite him would have to be the impetuous action of a girl who was already too close, and shaving him would give me that excuse, as well as getting him too aroused to refuse.

I did not have a plan for what was to happen after that, except that I would have to keep Gunnar out of the hold for several days. That would be next to impossible, as he was growing bored with the priest. That meant he would kill him soon, and go into the hold for another toy to play with. Any little thing could wreck my plan, and then Gunnar would probably kill us all.

But it was better than living on that cursed ship forever, having watched Claude-Michel suffer the terrible fate of being Gunnar's plaything. I would have rather died myself than see that.

The time came suddenly, two nights after my last attempt to feed. Gunnar turned the page of the book he was reading, made a face, and put it down. He swung his legs off the side of the bed and walked over to the corner where the young man lay huddled. "Time to meet your maker, Father," he said.

Predictably, the young man began to whimper and pray. I told myself I couldn't save everyone, and forced it out of my mind. Finally, they were gone. I leapt up, ignoring the feeling of nausea and the ache in my head that came with imagining Gunnar spilling the man's blood, and went to his toilette. The razor was out in plain view. I made sure it was closed, shoved it into my boot, and left.

Because the ship's cook was a kind man who liked me, I was able to get plates of meat and bread for Claude-Michel, François and Jean, instead of gruel. François opened his eyes but did not appear to see me, or the meal I placed beside him. Jean stared at his and sniffed. Claude-Michel watched me. "To what do we owe this banquet?" he asked, his voice tight.

"Eat first," I said. "Then I will shave you all." My heart beat much too quickly.

Claude-Michel brightened, then nodded. "Would you care to join us?" he asked.

Somewhere in the shadows, a rat squealed, making me jump. "No. Thank you, *Monsieur*," I said.

"What makes you decide to bring the razor, hmm?" he asked, and began to eat.

"You're very handsome," I answered, hoping against hope he didn't see how nervous I was. "I noticed in the beginning, when you first came, how handsome you were. Especially with your violin."

He nodded again. "*Merci, cherie,* but I will not be so handsome, I am afraid, when your Gunnar throws my entrails into the sea."

The image made my spirits sink. "Don't say such things."

I sat on the floor nearby, watching them. For a long time, no one spoke. Then, for some reason, I said, "My daughter, Annabelle, was four years old. The day before Gunnar's men came, she brought me a little purple flower. She said, 'Here, Mama. Pretty like you.' The baby was named for my husband, Philippe. He was a good man. Strong. But when the pirates came…" My throat closed around the words and tears came, but I wiped them away. "They killed him."

I tried not to sniff, but it was impossible. I wanted to show Claude-Michel vulnerability so he would trust me. I did not let myself think about what sort of life I was about to commit him to. At least, I reasoned, it would be a life.

Claude-Michel slowed his eating and listened.

I took a deep breath and tried to laugh, swiping a palm over my eyes and cheeks. "I tried to kill them when they hurt my babies. I tried. But then, I became afraid, and I ran. I should have made them finish me right there. This is Hell, this…remembering."

Claude-Michel swallowed too much, and coughed. "Perhaps there is something more for you still, some love you have not imagined, hm?"

I pretended not to hear. I could not afford to think about things like that, if what I was about to do may get both of us killed—or make Claude-Michel hate me forever.

Finally, he pushed away the plate. "I am ready," he said. He kept his eyes on me as I reached into my boot and drew out the blade. I went to him. For many moments, I could only stand there, looking down at him, very aware both Jean and Claude-Michel watched me intently. I wondered if I could go through with it.

"Well?" Claude-Michel asked. "Are you going to groom me or slit my throat?"

That brought me back. "I'm stronger than you," I said. "So don't try to do anything."

"As you wish," he answered.

Claude-Michel relaxed his hands on the floor and allowed the chains to go slack. I placed a boot on either side of his hips and lowered myself onto his lap. I felt embarrassed. I had never seduced a man before. "Very nice," he said.

"What?" I asked, alarmed.

"It's a very good perfume," Claude-Michel said. "There are not many pleasant smells in here, as you know."

I nodded and opened the blade, watching him carefully. Then, when I felt satisfied he wasn't going to try to kill me, I took his chin in my hand and turned his head to the side. In spite of the chains he moved quickly, and caught my wrists in his hands.

I met his eyes. "I cannot shave you unless you release me."

"I would rather shave myself," he said, attempting to pry my fingers from the razor's handle with his other hand. He could not.

"No, *Monsieur*. I will not give you the blade. And if you continue trying to take advantage of me I will go away and continue bringing you only gruel, and let you grow a hairy face like a madman until you die. It is a little comfort or none at all."

"Interesting," he muttered to my hand, as though he hadn't heard a word I said. "Perhaps the poison weakened me more than I realized."

"Yes," I said. "Perhaps. But I would like to make you feel like the man you are, not some animal in a cage. Now please, *Monsieur*, let me do what I came here to do."

He gave me a piercing look before dropping his hands to the ground and closing his eyes with a sigh. "At this point, *Mademoiselle*, I doubt it matters very much what you do."

"You did request that I shave you," I reminded him, maneuvering myself on his lap.

"If you continue to sit in this manner I will request something else as well," he said.

"I am not so talented to do both at the same time, *Monsieur*," I said, and placed the blade against his cheek. I had to close my mouth tight. I was becoming aroused, and my fangs were starting to grow, in spite of the nausea that came with imagining how his blood would taste. It did not help that I felt the flesh between his legs move beneath me.

God, how I wanted this man.

Claude-Michel closed his eyes and began to breathe deeply. I tried distracting myself with conversation. "Gunnar says the perfume is from the East. He has been everywhere. He is very old."

Claude-Michel let out his breath slowly.

"You're clenching your face, *Monsieur*. Please try to relax."

"My apologies," he said stiffly. "This is very nice."

It was all I could do to keep my hands from shaking. I was afraid he would notice, and know I had a plan. I didn't think he would enjoy knowing I was a vampire, or that I intended to make him one as well.

When I had finished, Claude-Michel's face was still rough, but the beard was gone. When I examined my work, I could see how handsome he was.

"*Merci,*" he said, and for a moment I thought he could hear my thoughts.

"You're welcome," I answered, allowing my desire for him to show through, and leaning forward for a kiss.

"Well," he said. "It seems the lady can't resist my charms."

"Don't speak," I said, and moved my hips against him. I wondered if he could feel the desperation in my touch. He raised his hands to grasp my derrière as my lips met his.

He returned the kiss briefly before turning his head. "I could be of better service, *Mademoiselle*, if my limbs were free."

I could tell he felt frustrated. Claude-Michel was not a man who enjoyed being at the mercy of others, even those trying to give him pleasure. I persisted, and held his jaw in place while nibbling his lip.

"*Mademoiselle...*"

"You will be free," I whispered, flicking my tongue against the corner of his mouth. "I promise." I moved my moist lips to his jaw, prickly where the razor had ripped at the beard stubble. His body stiffened as I probed his throat with my tongue. He gave an irritated sigh and took my arms in his hands, but was unable to move me much. I ignored the nausea raging through my gut and dug into the ground with my knees before forcing his head to the side.

Then I opened my mouth, and slid my teeth into his flesh.

I made my body rigid and closed my eyes tight, holding him against the wall. "What?" he cried and tried to throw me off of him. The taste of his blood made my guts lurch. I wanted to throw up, but I had to hold on, even though I knew I was hurting him. I had to save this man so he could save me.

Within moments, it was done. I stood up. His head lolled to the side as he tried to look at me. He spoke nonsense like a drunken man and could not pick up his hands from where they lay beside him, palms up. The last thing I wanted to do was bite another man, but I wanted to give Claude-Michel his friend, who was close to dying if something wasn't done. So I grasped the chains dangling from François' wrists in one hand and held them as I mounted him. Ignoring his weak, fevered struggles, I took a wad of his golden hair in my hand, forced his head to the side and lowered my mouth to his throat. "Shh," I said. "This will only hurt a little."

When it was over I saw that Jean watched me with wide eyes. He seemed unable to speak. When I crouched in front of him, he shrank away. "You will be food for your master," I said. "And we will all be free of this madman."

Chapter Seven

I HOPED to find Gunnar gone so that I could return his razor, but he was instead sprawled across the bed with his hands clasped atop his abdomen. I watched his breathing for several seconds to see if he was asleep. I decided he was, and hurried toward the toilette.

"Chloe."

When he spoke my name, I felt as though my entire body was on fire. I turned, hating the sound of it in his mouth. "Yes, Captain?"

"Come over here."

I hesitated. "I have to relieve myself," I said, which was not a complete lie.

He opened his eyes. "I guessed that already. Come over here now."

I wasn't sure whether my heart lurched because of the possibility of discovery or because of his tone, but I obeyed quickly, as always. "Yes, Captain," I murmured, praying he didn't want me naked.

He sat up as I approached, and looked at me appreciatively. He reminded me of a great white lion, with his broad features and shaggy mane. His musk was strong that night.

I did not wait for him to tell me to kneel between his legs and pleasure him. If I could satisfy him with my mouth, perhaps he would not insist on undressing me, and would not see the razor.

"Ahh…" he said as I encircled his member with my lips. "Very good. You have learned well since coming to me."

"Life is much easier when you're happy, Gunnar," I said before continuing.

"It is good you realize that," he said. "Take off your clothing. I want you to carry my juices in your belly tonight."

I stopped what I was doing and looked at him in horror. "But…"

"Why do you hesitate?" he asked. "And why are you suddenly so eager to please me?" He took my upper arms in his strong hands and picked me up as he stood, then walked over to the corner where he kept a flexible wooden rod. "Remove your clothing."

My mind raced while I unlaced my blouse. I moved slowly and tried to calm my thoughts, but Gunnar's return was swift. I felt the rod across my back before I could think. I stumbled and nearly went down, gasping loudly.

"Quickly," he said. "I don't know what you are hiding, but I do not intend to be manipulated."

I turned to him. "Please, Captain, don't," I said just as the rod struck again. This time, I went down in my knees, cowering. "Don't…"

"If I have to remove them for you, you will not wear clothes again on board this ship. Do I make myself clear?"

I nodded and stood, moving as quickly as I could with my trembling fingers. I pulled down my trousers and tried to use them to cover my right boot as I took it off, but the blade clattered onto the floor. Time stopped as I watched Gunnar's eyes narrow, and saw the recognition there. "What is this?" he asked, then grinned. "It will take much more than this to kill me."

I shook my head frantically. "I wasn't trying to kill you."

"Oh? Then please explain to me exactly what you were doing with my razor."

"I was…" I didn't want to tell him about shaving the prisoners, but in the end saw no other option.

"I just thought they were too weak to be dangerous," I finished. "It seemed a harmless kindness."

"No kindness is harmless," Gunnar said, making me stand, then moving around me like a cat studying its prey, periodically touching a nipple or a strand of hair, stroking a sensitive area. "Anyone for whom you feel compassion has a power over you, and will eventually use it." He moved close to my ear. "Do you know how old I am?"

I shook my head. "No," I said, trying to keep my voice steady. "You've never told me."

"I am over a thousand years old," he said. "The exact number of years, of centuries, I have walked this earth has ceased to be important. I am the last of a dead race. My native tongue no longer exists. I have been a man without a country, without even an epoch, for a very long time. I may as well be a god."

"It sounds very lonely," I said.

"Ah, loneliness." He touched my jaw lightly with his fingertips. It made me tremble. "Loneliness is the product of the lies we tell ourselves. As a priest among my people, I have had much time to discover what is necessary and what is not."

"Such wisdom and such cruelty together," I said. "How can a priest value life so little?"

He gave me a bitter smile. "The men who fall from great heights are those who sink the lowest."

"I will never understand you."

Gunnar pulled his hand away in a fist, as though catching something and crushing it. "It is a blessing then, that I don't crave your understanding. When you are as old as I, you realize that the society of others, the accolades of your fellow man, the love of a woman, are as the glistening snow, which disappears as soon as the weather turns. That it is far better to rely on the firmness of the ground beneath your own feet."

"But why do you enjoy destroying them?"

"Because I detest them—their weakness, their stupidity. If I find one worthy of my company, him I will spare."

"But your cruelty would turn him against you in the beginning."

"Perhaps," he said, nodding. "Perhaps I am destined to wander the earth until even the machinations of death bore me." For a moment he seemed to be in a reverie. Then, without warning, he dragged me over to the bed and took me mercilessly, opening my legs and driving into me painfully, holding my wrists down to the mattress. He watched my eyes the entire time, with a self-satisfied expression on his face. I looked up into his white eyes as he grunted into me, fearful he would read my plans in my eyes.

I tried not to become excited by his thrusting, but his weight on top of me and his cock finding the depths of my body never failed to make me want him, no matter how I nursed my hatred.

When it was over, he placed me in the chains he usually reserved for his dinner, shackling my hands and feet together and leashing me by the ankles to a bedpost so that I couldn't stand.

"In this manner," he said, "my people broke slaves. When a woman was finally given clothes and allowed to sleep on straw, she was grateful. Very grateful, indeed. I, myself, broke many slaves."

"Is that what I am to you?" she asked.

"Of course," he replied. "What else would you be?"

* * * *

Somehow, I slept.

I woke to the sensation of someone tugging on my chains and found one of Gunnar's men leering into my face, smelling of rum and feces. I started to break his nose, but noticed he had a set of keys and was about to unlock me. Outside Gunnar's cabin, there was chaos—the sound of cannons, heavy footsteps and shouting. The air smelled heavily of blood, gunpowder and fear.

"What is happening?" I demanded.

"We're being attacked," he said, running his disgusting, greasy gaze over my body. "The captain wanted me to get you out of these so you can die on your feet." He held the keys tightly and grabbed my bare breast. His hand felt rough and wet. The nails were blackened from years of filth.

"Good," I said.

There are moments in life when desperation becomes glorious, and this was one of those. The sound of a marauding vessel and the unyielding defiance I had seen in the dark eyes of the French captive combined with the pounding of my heart to give me the strength to seize this chance. I grabbed the pirate's wrist, breaking his arm at the elbow. He was too stunned to cry out, too stunned to do anything except gape at the odd way the limb now dangled. I broke his neck. Then I grabbed his sword and the keys, and worked as quickly as I could to unlock the heavy cuffs and chains.

Keeping the sword and keys near my hands, I dressed quickly and crouched beside the dead pirate to slip his dagger from its sheath and fit it into my boot, careful not to scratch myself with the dirty, crusty blade. I took such care more out of habit and disgust than necessity. With a sudden, violent scowl, I spat into his twisted features.

On deck, I looked this way and that for Gunnar, prepared to cut out his heart if I had to. I wondered if I would be physically able to do such a thing, and had no idea if he could even be killed. Fortunately, I did not see him. Other men crossed my path, however, but they were easy to kill. Later, I would be amazed at how easily I killed that night. It felt as though my body did the work while I watched from some faraway place.

In the confusion no one seemed to notice anything I did, including running a man through with the dead pirate's sword and taking his pistols. I put on the holsters and slipped a second dagger into my boot, then continued, sword ready, down to the ship's hold. I hadn't planned to take the prisoners out so soon, and did not even know if they were in any condition to make it, but this, I realized, was probably our only chance. If the invading ship's crew didn't kill us, then Gunnar would. And if he didn't kill me, he would see to it that there would be no more chances for escape. And my Frenchman would be gone forever.

"What's going on?" Jean cried as soon as I opened the door. I shushed him and looked at Claude-Michel, who watched me like a wild cornered beast. I had never seen a turning. With his sallow skin, sunken eyes, and limp hair he looked like a corpse glaring from the shadows.

I could barely tear my eyes away from him to speak to Jean. "If you want you and your master to make it out of here alive, you will do what I say," I growled. Jean looked as though he were about to start crying. His lip quivered. "Understand?" I repeated.

He nodded. "Yes, *Madame*."

I slid to my knees and unlocked him, then handed over my sword, instructing him to support François as I unchained him as well, all the while explaining that we were under attack and would have to swim for shore with the two men in tow. Claude-Michel muttered to himself.

"I can't swim," Jean said.

"Well," I answered. "Do your best."

When I reached for Claude-Michel's wrist cuffs, he snatched them away. "Get away from me," he said, and tried to sit up. Blood dribbled from his mouth as he spoke.

"Your new teeth are coming," I said as though it would make sense to him.

"I'll kill you," he returned, but made no move to prevent me removing his wrist cuffs a second time. "No one does these things to me."

"Perhaps you will kill me," I answered. "Or perhaps when you are stronger, you will thank me. For this moment, however, you will have to trust me," I said as his chains fell away. "Can you swim?"

He did not answer.

"Well," I said, freeing his ankles and hoisting him to his feet. "We'll see if you can. Either way, *Monsieur*, you are now free." I picked him up over my shoulders and nodded at François. "Do the best you can with him. We'll throw them overboard and jump in behind them. We'll have to keep their heads above water."

"What if I drown?" Jean asked.

"Then you'll probably die," I said. "But if you stay here, you will definitely die. Come on."

Because of his withered condition and my own vampire strength, Claude-Michel felt as light as a baby. I hoped François was unconscious and would not make things difficult for Jean. I did not expect all three of them to survive, but I would make sure Claude-Michel did, I told myself.

Up on deck, smoke hung in black clouds and made it difficult to see, even for me. Men shouted and cursed as the attackers boarded. Though I couldn't see them, I could hear their voices. They were Italians, perhaps pirates, or navy. I didn't care what they were, as long as they served as a decoy for me and my countrymen.

"Stay close!" I shouted at Jean and headed for the deck rail. I bumped a man through the smoke.

"What the...?" he exclaimed and whirled on me. I saw that it was the greasy Cockney. He grinned. "Oh, you're out, are you?" he said.

"*Oui,*" I replied, letting go of Claude-Michel, who slid to the floor. "I apologize, *Monsieur,*" I said as he scooted away. I didn't move my sword as fast as I should have. The Cockney sidestepped my aim, and thrust low. I felt pressure and heat in my left thigh. Even as thick, warm blood stained my trouser leg, I felt something else moving deep in the muscle, and knew it had already started to heal itself. The Cockney pulled his sword out of me, but not quickly enough to prevent me from opening his throat with my dagger.

I left him choking on the deck and got Claude-Michel to his feet. He glared at me but did not resist. Jean looked at me with something like awe and eyed my wound. "You'll bleed to death," he said.

"No, I won't," I told him. "Don't slip." We were only a few feet from the rail. Below us, the water rolled with the movement of the ships. "Swim," I whispered to Claude-Michel and helped him overboard. I turned to Jean. There was a splash below. Jean's eyes were wide. "That one too," I said quickly, nodding at François, who was unconscious again. I was very anxious to follow Claude-Michel, fearing the sharks would get him, or that he would drown.

Jean shook his head.

"Come on!" I shouted. "Your master is already out there! He needs us!" I pulled François out of Jean's grip and maneuvered him over the rail as well, then turned back to Jean.

"Put away your sword and jump," I said.

Again, he shook his head, brandishing his weapon at me. "I can't…"

"All right. But your master is in the ocean. If you want to be with him, you will have to follow me." I turned away, located Claude-Michel's flailing form, and leapt over the rail.

I caught him like a wriggling fish in my arms and held his head above the surface. Water sputtered from his mouth. "Jean…" he said.

"He's coming," I answered, but did not really think it was true. "But we have to find François." I scanned the surface but didn't see him. "Hold your breath," I said to Claude-Michel, looking at him intently. "Will you, please?" I asked.

Still glaring, he filled his lungs and moved with me under the water. I spotted François, caught beneath a slab of wood I had not noticed before. I had to leave Claude-Michel to tread water and go to François, tugging at him furiously and finally dislodging his blouse from jagged, splintery tears in the wood. His eyes bulged open. I felt sure he was dead. I placed him on top of the board with his arms dangling off the other side.

Claude-Michel half-swam toward me. Something exploded nearby, sending a tower of water into the air and causing us both to jump, but I managed to grasp Claude-Michel's slippery hands and arms and help him over to the board, where François' body dangled. "Hold on to this," I told Claude-Michel. "Stay with him. He needs you."

Claude-Michel gazed at François with a stricken look.

"He'll be all right," I said.

Something rose to the surface of the water and flailed in a death struggle. Hoping it was Jean, and that Claude-Michel would be able to hold on to the board, I took in a painful gulp of air and shot through the water. Limbs like octopus tentacles latched onto me, dragging me down. Because I knew I had very little chance of drowning, I was not afraid. I was able to take my time getting around behind Jean where I would be free of his cloying hands and could force him to the surface. He struggled like a rabid beast.

"Stop it!" I hissed into his ear as we broke the surface. "Stop it!" Water shot from his lungs and he threw up what was left of his last meal, gasping and looking around wildly. "It's all right," I said. "I have you. Your master's all right. Come on."

Somehow, I got him draped across the board. He looked around with quick eyes and flaring nostrils as though on the verge of another panic. I tried to calm him by petting his head.

"Calm down, boy," Claude-Michel said in the voice of an old man. "Or I'll..." He stopped and clutched at the board for his own life. "*Merde,*" he said, and looked at me desperately.

Chapter Eight

SOMEHOW, WE made it through the night. I found someone kind enough to take us in for a day so that I could find a room for us in the city, which I paid for with money I had taken from Gunnar's stash.

The two men slept on the bed while Jean took the couch. I hardly slept at all, but stayed up with Claude-Michel and François as though they were new babies. As soon as they were well enough to remain by themselves for a few hours, I decided, I would go into the street and find a new violin for Claude-Michel. This is the thought that kept my spirits up.

They slept silently, until three nights later, when Claude-Michel woke screaming. "Where am I?" he demanded. Jean was up like a shot, but it was up to me to press Claude-Michel back into the mattress. He looked skeletal, dry and gray. His eyes were sunken with purple bruising, and his teeth had fallen out. New teeth were forcing their way through his gums. He had already cut his tongue on his new fangs several times.

He calmed, then looked at me. "Vampire," he muttered.

"Shh," I whispered urgently. "You are becoming one too. We'll be in danger if you alert people."

"You did this to me," he hissed.

Behind him, François struggled as though trying to prop himself. He couldn't, so he settled for turning his head toward us. "Come on Claude-Michel," he said. "Stop being so temperamental. You wanted a way out, no?"

Claude-Michel lolled his head toward the other man's voice. François grinned at him—a terrifying pale visage with red, sunken eyes.

"Are you dead?" Claude-Michel asked. "You look terrible."

"But I've healed," François said. "Look."

Claude-Michel watched as François lifted his arm. The wound was inflamed and runny, but it had closed. "Impressive," Claude-Michel said.

"You will be fine in just a few days," I told them. "Then you will be ready to take food."

Claude-Michel gave me a distrustful look. "What kind of food?"

"You'll be ready for it when the time comes, " I said. "Trust me, you will want it then."

He nodded and settled back down onto the mattress, breathing heavily, sizing me up. "Who am I in danger of alerting, that his house is full of monsters?"

"The innkeeper. I had to persuade him that you and *Monsieur* Villaforte do not carry a plague. He finally agreed to give us one room with two beds so I could more easily care for you. I do not know how safe we are here."

"How long...?" Claude-Michel asked, then sighed.

"You have been sleeping for three days," I told him. "Do you remember being in the water?"

Claude-Michel closed his eyes and nodded as though it took all of his will to do it. "I remember," he croaked. "Barely."

"We were in the water all night. There was a shark, but I stabbed it in the nose."

"A shark," he said. "I must have slept. Where is Jean?" he asked, suddenly wide-eyed.

"I am here, *Monsieur*," Jean said softly, beside me.

Claude-Michel lifted a frail-looking hand in front of his face, flinching at the sight of scabs on his wrists where the metal cuffs had chafed. "I am only forty-four," he said. "These hands were strong...even a few days ago, they were strong."

I remembered how depressed I had felt at losing my beauty during the change. His sadness touched me. "They will be strong again," I assured him. I reached for his arm, but he recoiled and scowled. "Your hands will be stronger than they have ever been before," I said. "And you will never grow old, and you will not die. Is that not something to comfort you as you heal?"

"It sounds like a good trade to me," François said, closing his eyes.

Claude-Michel dropped his gaze for a second, then looked at me and did not flinch. For a moment, I felt happy at seeing the life in his eyes again. Then he spoke, and broke my heart again. "I think only of my dead children and wife. Until I kill the bastards who took their lives, there will be no comfort."

"Claude-Michel," François said. "We are free of that now."

"And today," Claude-Michel continued at me, ignoring him. "Today you tell me I will live with this grief forever? Without the release of death?"

"Perhaps you will change your mind when you are better," I said, standing.

"*Oui*," François agreed. "Forget this idea of revenge and embrace your new life, *mon ami*. We will be your new family. A family of beautiful monsters poised to take over the world."

I made myself smile for Claude-Michel's benefit. "I will return soon, *Monsieur*. It is still very important that you get your rest. There are difficult times ahead."

François turned his eyes to me. "What do you mean by that?"

"It means that our food will no longer wait patiently on our plates, François," Claude-Michel said, turning his back toward the other man. "We are altered forever."

* * * *

Over the next couple of days, their color improved and their teeth finished growing in. It is a painful process from which there was no relief at that time. But once the teeth are in, all the new vampire can think about is feeding. Claude-Michel reached this point before François.

He called me in a panic, wide-eyed and feral-looking. "Chloe!" He sat up and swung his legs over the side of the mattress.

Jean reached him first. "What is it, *Monsieur*?"

Claude-Michel gave him a look as though he were seeing a ghost. I recognized the light of first hunger in his eyes. Jean stepped toward him. Claude-Michel threw up his hand as if to ward off a demon.

"Stay back!" he growled.

I knew he was experiencing a hunger unlike anything he had ever felt, that he could hear the swish of blood in the boy's heart chambers, and that it inflamed his belly and loins. "Stay back!" he repeated. François watched him with an expression of horror.

"But *Monsieur*..." The boy looked crushed.

I sat next to Claude-Michel. "Don't worry," I told him. "Jean can provide food for all of us."

Claude-Michel's body became rigid. He turned to me with a look of disgust. But since I understood, and since I was relieved he was doing so well, I had to stifle the urge to laugh. "Jean? My Jean? I will not kill him," he said and pulled his hand away, getting slowly and awkwardly to his feet. I stood with him.

Jean backed away, wide-eyed. Claude-Michel was several inches taller now.

"You don't have to," I said. "Gunnar killed for pleasure, not out of necessity. What we need to do, it is nothing more than milking a cow. Feed from him, Claude-Michel. It is natural." I turn to Jean. "Come," I said. "Help your master."

"But..." Jean trembled visibly.

"Come on," I said. "He won't kill you. It will only hurt a little."

He nodded and took fragile steps toward Claude-Michel. I glanced over my shoulder to see how François was taking this. He watched, a fascinated expression on his face. Jean kept looking at me. I nodded encouragingly. Then Jean fixed a determined gaze upon his master and helped him sit on the mattress again.

It was Claude-Michel's turn to cast nervous glances at me. I smiled, even though the thought of seeing a feeding made me nauseated again. "Take your time," I said. "Find the vein."

Wild-eyed, Claude-Michel turned back to Jean, who now had to look up at him even though they sat side by side. He took Jean in his arms and guided him backward, lowering his head as if for a kiss upon his neck. He took in a big breath and I thought the smell must have washed over him, of blood, of warm flesh, of sex. He closed his eyes for a moment. Then he pressed his lips to the boy's neck, and probed gingerly with the tip of his tongue. During my first feeding, I had been unsure whether I knew what to feel for, but there it had been, that motion of blood beneath the skin and I had known, exactly, where to press the sharp tips of my fangs.

Jean let out a squeal like a caught mouse, but Claude-Michel clamped his hand over the boy's mouth and held him still. I knelt by the bed and held Jean's thrashing legs. Claude-Michel drove in his fangs a little too enthusiastically, causing Jean to scream into his hand. I felt badly for the boy, who was so very frightened, but I knew Claude-Michel would soon learn to make it pleasant for him.

I could not help but think of the warm, meaty taste of blood as I watched them. It was all I could do not to retch, but I didn't want to spoil this moment for Claude-Michel. It wasn't long before Claude-Michel pulled away. His lips had parted, and he looked down at Jean with a look that was both tender and bewildered. Jean's eyes, still frightened, were beginning to glaze over. He whimpered. Claude-Michel pet his cheek with the backs of his fingers. "Shh," he said. "I have finished."

When Jean nodded and closed his eyes, Claude-Michel looked back at me. I smiled. "My body wants to make love, but I am interested only in sleep."

"It is normal," I said. "You will want more later, but sleep is the best thing for you now. And for him."

Claude-Michel nodded and looked back at Jean, whose eyes looked far away. He snapped back to consciousness for a moment and regarded Claude-Michel curiously.

"What will happen to him?" Claude-Michel asked.

"He will become stronger, but he will not become what we are. Soon he will be able to provide us with much blood. We can survive with only him if we have to."

"But we will need more people?" Claude-Michel asked.

I nodded. "It would be best."

Claude-Michel struggled back into the bed. "My arms are tingling."

"Good," I said, helping Jean into the bed next to his master. "Get some rest." To François, I said, "You will be hungry soon."

* * * *

The next day, Claude-Michel was like a new man. He was propped on his elbow when I woke, leaning over his sleeping Jean and tickling his fingers through the boy's hair. I couldn't help but feel envious of the boy. After all, I had risked so much to save Claude-Michel, and I so wanted to feel his touch.

I put away those thoughts and got off the couch.

"How are you feeling?" I asked him.

The look of sheer joy he gave me made up for any jealousy I had felt for Jean. "I can see tiny things crawling on the walls," Claude-Michel said. "And hear the lovemaking of mice in their burrows. I am not sure that is a good thing."

"You will grow accustomed to it," I said with a smile, peering closely at his fingernails, which had grown quickly.

"Yes," he said. "I need a manicure."

"When you grow accustomed to your new hearing, you will listen only for what is important."

"I have not seen you dine," he said.

"I cannot dine on anything at the moment because my body is... Gunnar called it being 'in phase.' It is a time all vampires experience, losing their appetites so that they will not accidentally create other vampires. Only in this time will the bite transform."

"How often does this happen?"

"I don't know. Not very often. Gunnar seemed surprised it had happened to me so soon. I have not been—I have not been a vampire for very long."

Claude-Michel lifted his fingers toward my face. "I am grateful," he said. "I feel better than I have ever felt before."

I smiled. "I am glad."

"I want to stand up," he said, and sat up on the edge of the bed. Jean shifted, but was sleeping deeply. I glanced at François, whose eyes were open just a sliver.

I tried to help Claude-Michel stand, but he waved me away. "I am not an old man," he snapped. He shuffled forward a few steps. He looked like a drunk man.

"It will be difficult to move around at first," I said. "You are several inches taller than you were. The growth causes pain, but that will go away in a few days."

"I'm taller?" he asked.

"Yes, *Monsieur*," I said. "You are a different kind of man now. A different creature. More than a man."

It was at that precise moment that my eyes wandered too far and noticed the bulge between his legs. I looked away quickly, blushing. But he noticed. He cocked his head and grinned at me.

"I think it is time I see what a vampire's body is capable of," he said.

My heart leapt at the thought of finally feeling his touch. I returned his smile, but he turned to the sleeping boy. I lowered my head, grateful he had not seen the tears pricking my eyes. But François saw. He watched silently from his spot on the bed. I thought I detected a hint of satisfaction in the way his eyes gleamed. Glaring at him, I threw myself onto the couch.

In spite of my disappointment, I was fascinated by Claude-Michel's lack of inhibition as he opened Jean's breeches and tugged them over the boy's slender hips. I wanted to be him so badly. Jean came to quickly and whimpered.

"Are you frightened?" Claude-Michel asked when the boy was half-nude.

Jean nodded quickly. Claude-Michel pet his hair in long strokes. "It is all right," he said. "I am still your master."

"You're taller," Jean said.

"But do I appear different?" Claude-Michel cooed.

Jean nodded again. "You look... more alive," he said, then turned his head on the pillow like a sleepy angel. "I don't know what I'm saying."

Claude-Michel chuckled. "I am sure you know more than you think. Now, I am going to enjoy you, and you are going to obey me, as always. Yes?"

Jean turned back to him and nodded. "Yes."

He did not look at his master as Claude-Michel tested the strength of his senses, finding all of his favorite spots on Jean's body with his nose, and with his fingers. I found my own fingers searching out my body, moving down between my legs as I watched the spectacle. I began to pant as Jean began to pant with Claude-Michel's attentions, until his master opened his own breeches and ordered the boy on his stomach while François lay on his side, watching them with glittering eyes. Claude-Michel pressed his body against the body of his servant and kissed his neck tenderly, whispering, "*Cher*," over and over in a husky growl. I wanted that voice in my own ear. I wanted to close my eyes tightly and give myself to it, but forced my eyes to stay open, to watch what Claude-Michel did, and learn how he made love.

Heat spread from where my fingers worked between my legs, down my thighs and into my belly as Claude-Michel ordered Jean on all fours. The boy obeyed quickly, but cried out when his master pressed into him all at once.

Claude-Michel did not know the full extent of his strength. On several occasions, Jean whispered, "You're killing me, *Monsieur*." Several times, Claude-Michel slowed his pace, all the while gripping the boy's hips and pulling him back to meet his loins, leaving imprints that would no doubt soon turn into bruises.

Chapter Nine

NEXT MORNING, François and Jean watched while Claude-Michel inspected a pile of clothing I bought the day before from a nearby shop. "It is very strange," Claude-Michel said, "that the landlord has not come in to say hello, considering the pathetic state in which we arrived."

"But he has come," I said. "While you were sleeping. The second day we were here."

François and Claude-Michel looked at each other.

"While we were sleeping?" Claude-Michel echoed. "And you allowed him in?"

"It is his inn, *Monsieur*," I said quickly.

"While we rent it, it is ours," he said, spitting out the word "rent" as though it were something filthy.

François propped himself on one elbow and tried to appear awake. His teeth were in and he had enjoyed his first feeding only hours before. Jean slept soundly next to him on the bed.

"I did not want to alarm him," I said. "He's already concerned over what kind of disease you might have."

"What did you tell him?" Claude-Michel asked, having forgotten the breeches in his hand.

"I told him, simply, that being chained in a dungeon had weakened you." That is when I happened to look at François, who was watching me strangely. There was a curious intensity in his blue eyes that worried me. I looked away and tried not to think about it, but my eyes returned to him within seconds. He was still staring at me, so I turned to Claude-Michel.

"I would ask you, *Monsieur*..." I said to Claude-Michel. "You will soon feel like the strongest man in the world. But it would be best, perhaps, if you did not act like it."

Claude-Michel nodded and put down the breeches, approaching me slowly, grinning like a young man. "A ruse of weakness."

"Yes, *Monsieur*. Unless we leave immediately, but—" I paused as he reached out to lay his hand alongside my jaw. My heart hammered in my breast. I wondered if I dared to hope he could want me, but had to make sure he understood the predicament we were in. "I don't know how to be in the world. Not as we are."

"Very carefully," he said, looking into my eyes. "We will need to stay here for a little while at least. I wish to make some inquiries in town about an old friend."

François sighed loudly.

"A friend?" I asked.

"Yes," Claude-Michel answered.

"Perhaps if you tell me who it is, I can find out for you while I am out this morning.'

"You're going out again?" François asked. Claude-Michel glanced over his shoulder at him, then returned to me with an inquisitive expression.

"Yes," I said. "I can't wait until you are fully recovered before I seek out additional sources of food. And I don't want to exhaust Jean."

Claude-Michel nodded and pulled away, returning to the clothing. "I see. No, there is no need to do anything other than what you have planned."

I could feel my brow furrow, and wondered if I had angered him somehow. I tried to smile, knowing without a doubt that he would love having a violin again. "I will return by midday. You should be ready to travel in perhaps two days."

"It will be interesting to look upon the world with new eyes," Claude-Michel said to the clothing.

I made my way to the door, and lingered for a moment to see if François was still watching me—he was—and then left.

They began talking when I reached the stairs. I went halfway down and stopped to listen.

"Do you think she is telling the truth, Claude-Michel? About looking for new people?"

"Perhaps she is lying," Claude-Michel answered. "But I can think of nothing she would gain by it."

I listened tensely. I wondered why he didn't defend me to Francois. After all, I had risked my life to save them.

"Perhaps she is planning to shop," Claude-Michel finally said.

"Do you think she is leaving holes in people all over the village?" François asked, laughing. I could tell by the way his voice changed that he was now up and moving around the room. There was a derisive tone in his laughter I didn't like.

I heard Claude-Michel sigh. "I don't know what she's doing, but I'm sure she will share it with us once we're ready to join her. Why are you suspicious? She is our rescuer after all."

"I was under the impression that we vampires kept chattel. It will be difficult to keep our secret if she is roaming the streets eating everyone. Besides, she doesn't know what she's doing. She as much as said it herself. That man had her on that ship for many months. He did not teach her how to survive."

"She knows what she's doing."

"What if she doesn't come back?" François continued.

"What do you mean?" Claude-Michel asked. "Not a single mirror in this place," he muttered.

"What if she decides we're too much trouble, and abandons whatever plan she had for us—and us as well? Like it or not, she is everything we have to learn from."

"We don't need this girl to take care of us. Why don't you try to take a little more nourishment from Jean, eh? You will feel better once you're on your feet."

François did not reply. I was about to leave when I heard him say, "Who, may I ask, could you be dreaming of visiting here?"

"Katarina," Claude-Michel said softly. "I want to find her."

All the breath left my body at the sound of another woman's name. I felt crushed, certain I meant nothing to him.

"That Gypsy whore?" he asked, incredulously. "Why, Claude-Michel?"

"That Gypsy whore," Claude-Michel answered in slow, even tones, "has been with me since I last said goodbye to her. Always, I have had her father's violin with me to remind me of that time. Now even that is gone. But so are any reasons I once had to resist seeking her out."

"She's probably dead by now, Claude-Michel. If not, then she's an old hag. What use could you have for an old woman?"

"I want to see her," Claude-Michel said. "And I will find her."

François nodded. "If it is what you wish," he said.

I left then, dazed. My earlier excitement about finding a violin for Claudio had disappeared, and I began to think maybe it was best if I did make plans to leave them.

Chapter Ten

FOR A while, I simply walked the streets with a lump in my throat. All of my vampire sight could not help me see through the tears that were forming in my eyes. I knew, however, I could not let them fall. I could not show such weakness in the street. A woman alone would attract attention. I knew I could take care of myself, but what then? What if I was discovered to be a vampire?

Gunnar's threats to leave me in the first village he came to returned. I wondered how much danger I was in. Then I realized I didn't care. With my family gone and the man I pinned my hopes on disinterested in me, I had no one. There was no reason to live.

I decided I would stay with Claude-Michel and François for a few months to ensure they knew how to survive. I remembered how Claude-Michel looked at me in the hold and new tears formed. Then I remembered the sound of his playing. He needed a violin, I told myself, even if he didn't need me. I began my search.

It was midday before I found any sort of violin at all. A young man was playing it for money in the square. It sounded beautiful, so I approached him. At first, he did not want to part with it. I offered him almost all the gold I had brought with me—enough to feed him for a week and purchase another instrument. He could not resist, even though he gave his instrument one last, longing look as he placed it in the hemp cloth he carried it in and handed it to me. I gave him the coins and began my journey back to the inn, which was another hour's walk.

My success brightened my spirits, and I allowed myself to hope—not for Claude-Michel to love me, or even want me, but for him to be pleased with me for just a little while. Then I could pretend things were different than they were, just until the next day, when I would begin to make plans for living on my own.

* * * *

Things were not quite as I expected when I returned. It was mid-afternoon, and Claude-Michel was very, very angry.

He met me at the door. François was on his feet, and looking much better than usual. Jean sipped a glass of wine on the couch. But it was Claude-Michel who kept my attention. He worked his jaw and flared his nostrils angrily. His black eyes flashed as they had when Gunnar broke his violin.

"Claude-Michel…?" I asked hesitantly.

"Put that down," Claude-Michel said, motioning with his head toward my packages.

I tried to smile, thinking perhaps I had read him wrong. "I apologize, *Monsieur*, for taking so long. It was a strange errand and I wasn't sure where to begin, but I think you will enjoy—"

He stepped toward me. "I said, put that down."

"Claude-Michel..." I began, but faltered. I swallowed and hurried toward the bed, and placed everything there.

"Put it on the floor," he said.

I searched his face, wondering how he could be so angry and what I might have done, but I didn't dare ask. I looked at Jean, who looked from me to Claude-Michel uncertainly. Then I made the mistake of looking at François, who flung himself on the mattress and grinned. "I do so love the theater," he said.

I tried to keep my lip from trembling as I did what Claude-Michel said.

In mere seconds he had my arm and was pulling me toward the bed. "Claude-Michel...what...?" But in another moment, I was bent over his knee with my skirts raised. "Why are you doing this?" It was more of a panicked cry than a question.

He did not answer. He simply began bringing his hand down hard on my *derriere* until tears spilled from my eyes. He spoke between clenched teeth. "When you say you will return at midday, you will return at midday, not several hours later. Do you understand?"

All I could do was nod frantically and gasp. "Please, Claude-Michel..." I begged, holding a fistful of his breeches leg in my hand, yelping in pain and surprise.

"Don't cry out," he warned.

I obeyed, not wanting to make him even angrier. I could not stop whimpering, or keep my body from heaving with a steady stream of sobs. "Please..." I gasped, whenever I was able to catch my breath.

Claude-Michel stopped only when he had spanked me enough so that the pain would be with me for several days, in spite of my capacity for healing. At first, I could do nothing. He allowed me to slowly struggle to my feet. My movements caused me to cry out. I looked at him quickly, afraid he would strike me again for it. My skirts fell around my hips and legs as I stood.

"Look at me," Claude-Michel said sharply. I obeyed. He stood.

"First, I forbid you to go on such errands without my permission," Claude-Michel said. "Second, if you don't return in what I consider a reasonable time," he said, with a tight smile, "the next time it will not be my *hand* on your derriere."

I swiped at an escaping tear with shaking hands.

"I worried terribly, *cherie*," he said, reaching for me. I cringed away, confused, but he only brushed strands of hair from my face. "I thought perhaps you had been killed, and I have just found you. I did not want to lose you so soon." He lifted my chin, and made me meet his eyes. I nodded, still confused. I hardly understood what he was saying.

"I am sorry, *Monsieur*," I said, as my eyes filled with new tears.

"Now," he said. "What was so important that you had to spend most of the day accomplishing it?"

I pulled away and went to the hemp-wrapped bundle, picked it up and presented it to him. At first, there was curiosity on his face. Then his brow furrowed as he unwrapped it. He drew out the violin slowly, his eyes widening in surprise. A bow fell to the floor at his feet.

"Where did you get this?" he asked.

I was afraid to answer, in case what I said earned me further punishment. "I wanted to find one I thought suitable for a man of your standing," I said, hurrying to pick up the bow. "Sometimes those of noble birth find themselves in hard times and are willing to sell such things for little money, but sometimes it is difficult to find. I bought it from a boy in the square. I paid too much for it, I know, but I wanted you to have it so badly…"

His thumb brushed the scroll as he stared at it. *"Merci,"* he said quietly.

That evening, Claude-Michel sent Jean out for food for himself, and enough wine for everyone. I had told him Gunnar still appreciated whiskey and rum, and he wanted to test his own palate.

For the first time since moving into the room, I went out on the balcony. It was a small balcony, overlooking dirty streets. But it was better than continuing to look at the walls. Claude-Michel came to find me, lounging against the doorframe. "My dear, sweet Chloe," he said. "My new violin is one of the most finely crafted instruments I have seen. How did you find such a thing?"

I turned only enough so that I could see him. From the corner of my eye, I noticed François watching us from the couch, trying not to be seen. "If you think I stole your money to purchase it, I did not," I said. "I purchased it with money I took from Gunnar. I thought it would buy us rent or clothes, but you seemed in need of something to do with your hands."

"It is lovely," Claude-Michel said. "I thank you very much, *cherie*."

I could not answer. I did not know if I could trust the warmth in his voice.

He continued. "You saved us. Do you know this? You are a very brave girl."

Still, I could say nothing. Without warning, Claude-Michel closed the gap between us with inhuman speed, startling me. "Apparently, I have many strange new abilities," Claude-Michel said. "Are there more surprises?" He smiled down at me with boyish glee, and for a moment, my heart was lifted. Still, I thought perhaps he was trying to keep me friendly until he had no further use for me, or that he felt guilty for making me cry, and my heart sank again.

"Perhaps the surprises will be for me, *Monsieur*," I replied. "Yesterday, looking from place to place, I was very excited to think how pleased you would be when you saw your new violin. I lost track of time. Time passed, and I could not find what I wanted. Then I lost my way. Thoughts of you, and of our new freedom, kept me from becoming too frightened. Now I wish I had never seen that terrible violin."

"No, Chloe, no," Claude-Michel said, and took me in his arms. I felt startled and confused, but he did not let me escape. "It is a beautiful instrument. Simply beautiful, and I will treasure it always." He looked down into my eyes, and spoke with heartbreaking gentleness. "But you must know what kind of man I am. I am passionate about all things that are important to me. Do you understand? You have become important to me. I was sick with terrible imaginings, *cherie*, of terrible things that could have happened to you. It was not good that you stayed so long. For that, I am very displeased."

My lips opened, but I did not know what to say. My heart began to flutter wildly.

"But I am very pleased that you wanted to give me a violin," Claude-Michel said.

"You spanked me...like a child."

"Yes," he said. "I punish disobedience. I make no apologies."

I nodded, but said nothing. Then Claude-Michel kissed me and I could not help but relax in his arms as those lips covered mine. I heard François groan from the couch and wondered what he was doing. The next moment, my fangs began to grow. I felt the rhythms in my body shift.

I did not have to wonder for long what François was up to. When Claude-Michel guided me to the empty bed, François did not even make an attempt to take his hand away from his crotch. He watched me with a lecherous half-smile on his lips. But I determined not to think about him then. Claude-Michel wanted me. That was all that mattered.

Claude-Michel murmured as he began to undress me. "I have taken only two others as I am about to take you," he said.

"What do you mean?" I asked, suddenly worried. Gunnar had had strange tastes in the bedroom that were not always pleasant. I wondered if Claude-Michel did as well. And I tried not to notice François opening his breeches. I hoped he didn't come over to us. I wondered what I would do if Claude-Michel wanted to share me with him.

When I was nude and lying splayed on the mattress before him, Claude-Michel began to reveal his beautiful body. My eyes followed the pattern of hair on his chest and the dark line down into his breeches. When he took them off, his erection sprang forth, and I became afraid, as though I was a virgin again.

It must have shown on my face. "Shh," he said, nestling between my legs, letting the warmth of his shaft press against me, kissing my face. I could see his fully extended fangs as he spoke. *What a magnificent vampire he makes*, I thought.

The morning mist had caused a curl to form at Claude-Michel's cheek, which gave him a slightly boyish look. I reached up to touch it. He smiled at me and reached down between his legs to position his erection, preparing to penetrate me.

"Many women have given themselves to me," Claude-Michel said, moving his the slick head of his erection over me. "And beautiful boys, also."

"I know the reputations of nobles, *Monsieur*," I said.

"And now, I assume I will live for a very long time, yes?"

I nodded. "Yes."

"So I will take many, many more." His words caused a pain in the middle of my chest. "But not in the way I am about to take you. I take them in the pleasure of the moment. But you are so much more than that, my dear."

I looked into his eyes.

"You, I wish to keep," he murmured. "Open for me, my dear, my Chloe. I will show you pleasure like no one else ever has, or ever will again."

I let out a long groan as the length of his erection slid inside of me. "You belong to me now," he whispered. "My Chloe."

Tears slid out of my eyes as he rocked his hips gently. He filled me and stretched me, making my body want him. I was torn between throwing my arms around him and looking into his beautiful face. He twined his fingers in mine and held me in place, breathing heavily as he pressed into me over and over.

While this was happening, I heard the slick, wet sounds of François pleasuring himself. For some reason, his soft grunts heightened my own excitement. Before long, the heat and pressure between my legs became agonizing. Then release came, and I quivered in Claude-Michel's arms. At first, I did not know what had happened to me. I had never had an orgasm before.

As I lay dazed and breathless, Claude-Michel pounded into me mercilessly, driving my body to writhe beneath him. I whimpered with the pain and pleasure of his thrusting. He sounded like an animal. Then he paused, and then fucked me harder still, finally shoving his cock into me as far as it would go and letting out a long groan of release. I could feel him throbbing inside of me.

He lowered himself to his elbows and kissed me. "My dear Chloe," he murmured. After several moments of this I realized François had grown quiet. I ignored him when he got up to clean himself.

"You are a very beautiful woman, Chloe," Claude-Michel said. "One who should be enjoyed by someone who appreciates beauty. Not by a man like Gunnar."

"Gunnar appreciates nothing," I said darkly.

"You will never have to think of him again."

"Who are the other women?" I asked suddenly.

"What other women, *cherie*?" Claude-Michel asked.

"The two other women you took like you took me."

Claude-Michel nodded with an expression of understanding. "My wife is one," he said.

For some reason, the mention of Claude-Michel's wife made François stop in the middle of what he was doing and look at us. In spite of myself, I met his eyes. He looked away quickly and went out on the balcony. Even then, I thought this most strange.

"*Was* one," he corrected himself. "She is dead. The other is Jean, not a woman at all. You are one of three I ever intended to keep forever."

"Oh," I said. "I am sorry about your wife."

"Yes," he said, and rolled over onto his back, gazing at the ceiling. He did not speak again for a while. Then, quietly, as if to himself, he said, "We must leave this place soon. Our money is running out, yes?"

I nodded.

"This evening, you will remain here with Jean. Do you understand? You will not leave this room."

"But why—"

"François and I will go out and find additional food."

"But you can't. You don't know how."

"I know how to hunt, *cherie*, even if I have never done so as a vampire. We will bring someone back with us and use her here."

I grew silent. I did not like the idea that they would bring a woman here and do things with her right under my nose. But I understood even then that a man like Claude-Michel would not be faithful to one woman alone.

"Perhaps there will be a gentleman in need of parting with his fortunes as well," he said.

"When will you go out?"

"At dusk, when the desperate emerge from the safety of their homes. When alcohol makes men's tongues loose. We must also find a way to leave this place."

"Leave?" I said. "But you have only just turned, and it is the first place we've been safe—"

"We can not stay here," Claude-Michel said. "We are running out of money and Jean is not enough. And there are people I must find."

"People?" I asked. "Who?" I remembered the conversation I had overheard about the Gypsy woman, but I wanted to hear what he would say.

In the pause that followed, a darkness crossed Claude-Michel's face. It caused my scalp to prickle. I was afraid to push him too far. "The bastards who killed my wife and daughter. I have every intention of making them pay."

I shook my head. "No. Claude-Michel...no...".

"Every night I close my eyes and dream of hurting those men. It must be done."

"France?" I asked.

"Yes, for a time." Claude-Michel turned to me and smiled sadly, touching my face with the backs of his fingers. "But first we enjoy Italy, no?"

I nodded. It did not matter that Claude-Michel was a complicated man. He wanted me with him. I would not have to fend for myself. I smiled and drew close to him, putting my head on his chest and closing my eyes.

Before drifting off to sleep, I thought I heard François hiss the name, "Katarina."

Chapter Eleven

THAT EVENING, as Jean combed Claude-Michel's hair, I fussed with his coat while he sat in the chair for the writing-desk. The coat was scarlet-and-gold, and I had bought it for him the day I bought the violin. It fit remarkably well, considering I guessed at his size. I didn't have quite the same luck with François' coat, which was a little small in the shoulders. In addition, he didn't like the color.

"It's cream," he said, examining his reflection in the wall mirror. "It fails to show off my crown of golden locks and makes me look...yellow. Powder blue, on the other hand, would light up my eyes nicely and give me a more... angelic visage."

He looked over his reflection's shoulder, at Claude-Michel sitting while Jean tied his hair back with a black satin ribbon. François grunted.

"Well, your golden crown is a mess," Claude-Michel said. "You've done nothing but complain, and it's nearly dark."

"This is what happens when you take all the servants for yourself," François said, grinning right at me. I pretended not to see, and turned my attention back to Claude-Michel's coat. I was already beginning to wish I had left François on Gunnar's ship. Claude-Michel motioned for me to step aside, which I did, a little hurt that he neither thanked me for my attention to his appearance nor looked at me. He simply stood and went to the mirror.

"No powder," he said. "Still, I will be difficult to resist, yes?"

"You should be able to convince some desperate creature to return with you," I said. He didn't respond.

François looked him over. "Are you finished?"

"Yes," Claude-Michel said, turning away with a flourish of his hand. "You may borrow the servants. I will wait for you downstairs. Remember: The longer you keep me waiting, the more of our money I will spend on wine."

Claude-Michel's use of the word "servants" caused my chest to hurt. I expected as much from François, but not from the man who had wooed me so relentlessly just a few hours before. I had not yet learned of his love of the dramatic moment, or his carelessness. I swallowed hard, trying to make the feeling go away, as I moved toward the bed, careful to keep my back to the men so they couldn't see the confusion I knew must be etched across my face.

"Has he always been so arrogant?" I asked when he was gone.

François took long strides to the chair in front of the dressing table and made himself comfortable. Jean dutifully picked up the comb.

"No," François said to him. "I want her to do it."

"As you wish," Jean replied.

I turned to find François grinning at me again. Rage tightened my chest. "Come on," he said. "Are you waiting for my golden crown to become a silver one? Oh, but that will never happen, will it?" he asked, delighted with himself.

I had to set my jaw for this. I went to him quickly and accepted the comb from Jean. I stood behind François as though I would do as he asked, and took his tangled locks in one hand.

"You know," he said, "I have known Claude-Michel a long time, pussycat. A long time. I know him much better than you ever will."

"Is that so?" I asked, working out the tangles much more roughly than was necessary. "What makes you think I care?"

He clicked his tongue. "Really, *cherie*, you should remember who your betters are."

White-hot anger moving from my chest and down both arms made me stop combing. Before I realized what I had done, I was holding a wad of François' hair in my hand and pulling back his head as though I would slit his throat. At that moment, I would have enjoyed doing exactly that. "I am your maker," I snarled in his ear. "Some would say that grants me the right to respect."

For a moment, François did not respond. Then he said, "You're right, of course. Are you finished with your display?"

I let go slowly. The next thing I knew, he had whirled on me, taken me across the room and pinned me to the bed. His blue eyes seemed a darker shade as he regarded me hotly. His voice came out in a snarl. "You lost any claim of power here when Claude-Michel spanked you like a child.

Do you think he would give an argument if I did the same after what you've just done?" He snorted.

I fought to hold on to my righteous anger, but fear had already dampened its edges. I hated that the mere mention of a spanking was enough to make me lose my resolve. For a moment, I looked away. Then I forced myself to return my gaze to his. By that time, however, an expression of triumph had come over his face. He released me with a look of disdain. "You cannot come between us," he said, straightening his coat. "No one can."

I did not dare move, did not even dare to breathe deeply. Tears of shame stung my eyes. I tried not to let him see me tremble.

"Now," he said quietly. "Comb my hair."

I felt as though something in me had deflated. I did what he said, because I did not know how to do anything else. I did not want this man to spank me. I did not want to learn to fear him. But that is what was happening. My hands shook. Not another word was spoken between us until François once again stood in front of the mirror, his hair pulled back with a black ribbon like Claude-Michel's.

"I supposed it's as good as I can hope for until you're trained," he said, turning back to me. "Now remember what Claude-Michel said. Stay in this room and take your meal from Jean tonight."

"Of course," I said. I could not even feel anger at the command.

"We will return late," he said. "Do not bother to wait for us."

I held my breath as I watched him go, then held still and listened to his feet in the hallway outside. Only then did I allow myself even to swallow hard. I went to the washbasin. I wished Jean was not there, so I could cry. Instead, I would have to wait until the small hours of the morning while everyone else slept, and I would have to be quiet. Resigned to what the day had become, I undressed while Jean straightened the room.

"I am glad you got this for him," he said from the corner where the violin had been placed. "He enjoys playing more than he will admit."

"Yes," I said. "I thought so." I stood bare-breasted at the basin, my dress hanging from my hips, and ran the cool washcloth up my arm.

"Are you frightened?" Jean asked suddenly.

It startled me. I looked up. "What?"

"Are you frightened you'll be punished?"

I looked into the water, hating everything. "I have been already. Claude-Michel did it when I returned yesterday."

Jean came over and sat on the edge of the bed, near me. "He punishes me too."

"And Monsieur Villaforte?" I asked. My words felt like a challenge, though I hadn't intended them to be. I wondered how often I would get myself into trouble with Claude-Michel thanks to unintended challenges.

"I have only seen him strike someone when Monsieur du Fresne wanted to see it," Jean said, apparently without noticing my tone. "Perhaps it will not happen."

"It would not surprise me if Claude-Michel wanted to see it. He was so cold this evening. I thought..." I could not finish, and instead bit my lip. I squeezed water from the cloth and washed my shoulder. "You're right," I said finally. "I am frightened."

Jean stood and reached around me for the cloth, startling me again. "May I, Mistress?"

My eyes widened momentarily. I hated the pounding in my breast, told myself this was just a boy. Then I remembered he was probably older than I was, and he was asking for control, even though the word "mistress" rolled easily off his tongue. Torn between giving up the control I had over just one person, and the promise of feeling this boy's gentle touch, I hesitated.

Finally, I relented and handed over the cloth. "Thank you," I said.

His touch was feather-light as he moved the damp cloth over my skin. I shuddered at the way it felt, bowed my head and closed my eyes. The contrast between my treatment this evening and how Claude-Michel had made love to me just a few hours before made me feel terrible. How could he have taken me so attentively and then turned his back on me to go hunt for whores? I did not realize I was crying.

"Am I doing it too hard, Mistress?"

I looked at him over the shoulder of my reflection. "No, Jean."

"You shouldn't have pulled his hair," he said.

"Yes, I know," I whispered, shivering as the cloth traveled down the length of my back, resting for a moment at the top of my *derriere*, before starting over again.

"I'm to feed you tonight," he said, his tone mildly suggestive.

I said nothing, but simply allowed him to touch me and caress me with the cloth, wondering what it would be like when Claude-Michel and Francois returned.

I had not expected to sleep tangled in the bed sheets with Jean, but found myself waking with a start when Claude-Michel and Francois came in with a tipsy prostitute.

Chapter Twelve

I SAT up quickly when the door opened, startling Jean. Except for scant covering by the sheets, we were completely nude. All of a sudden, I wondered if Claude-Michel would be angry with me for making love with his boy. My heart pounded relentlessly when I saw he was carrying a riding crop he had not had before. He tossed it on the bed near me. I felt ill.

Jean leapt out of bed and grabbed his trousers. "I am sorry, *Monsieur*. I should have been waiting for your return." His beautiful honey-colored hair was mussed.

"I have plenty to keep me occupied for a while." I could tell by the way Claude-Michel smiled his fangs were extended. He was being careful not to let them show. I pulled the sheets around me and glared at François, who gave me a smug smile.

Even though the sight of Claude-Michel with another woman made me uneasy, I could not look away. I was fascinated by how the two men surrounded her. In spite of their arrogance, they were both very beautiful. I wondered in that moment what it would feel like to be in her place.

"Sit with me, Jean," I whispered.

He shook his head. "I must remain ready in case my master should need me."

"I don't think he's going to," I said crossly and curled up in the sheets to watch.

Claude-Michel cleared his throat and took the girl's wrap slowly from her shoulders, then handed it to Jean, who placed it on the back of the chair. Claude-Michel placed his hands on the girl's bare shoulders and spoke seductively. "I think our servants have worn themselves out. This one, however, is not yet used up," he said, sliding his fingers into her hair.

I could see the feeding hunger in François' eyes. I wondered how long he could control himself before he threw down the prostitute and raped her with his fangs.

"We must make sure we get everything we've paid for, yes?" François said.

She gave him a coy smile. "I will please *Signore* in every way possible."

"Yes, you will," Claude-Michel said, guiding her toward the bed, which horrified me. In my disturbed fascination, I did not consider they might want the bed. "And perhaps find another way after that."

I pulled my legs away from them and scrambled to the headboard as the girl climbed onto the bed and got on her knees to help Claude-Michel remove his coat. François removed his own coat, hastily. Jean took it, and Claude-Michel's as well. When the girl turned and went for François's blouse, Claude-Michel took her wrists in his hands.

"No," he whispered. "I paid for your body. I want to see it." His words were almost a snarl. They sent a bolt of heat through my stomach and caused me to tingle between my legs.

The girl nodded and tried to tug away her wrists, but Claude-Michel pulled her from the bed and held her tight against him, pressing his crotch to her bottom. "No, my dear. Monsieur will do it." With that, he brought her arms behind her back, where he held them with one hand. Before she had time to protest, he clamped a hand over her mouth.

"Shh," he whispered in her ear. "You will not be hurt tonight… much. And you will be well paid." To François, he said, "Try out your new strength. Rip it from her." He had a wolfish glint in his eye.

For the first time that evening, the girl looked worried. "It is all right, my dear. We only want to play just a little rough, yes?"

She nodded uncertainly.

"Good," he said. "François."

I could not help but be fascinated as François pushed his fingers down into the girl's bodice and gave one forceful tug as Claude-Michel pulled her body backward. The girl squealed into Claude-Michel's hand as the front panels of the bodice separated from the back and her blouse went limp against her freed breasts. The girl yelped in surprise.

Claude-Michel released the girl. She looked at me, frowned, and turned back to Claude-Michel with an uncertain smile. She dropped to her knees and began to unfasten his breeches. He let her. François sat on the mattress behind her with a lazy smile on his face, head propped on one hand, watching the girl pleasure his friend.

Jean stood nearby, watching dispassionately, ready in case his master needed anything.

Claude-Michel put his fingers in her hair and threw his head back. I could see the tips of his fangs. After a while, François got up and moved around behind him, slowly pulling the bow out of Claude-Michel's ribbon and tugging it out of his hair, touching his friend's dark locks sensuously with parted lips. His fangs were extended as well. Claude-Michel hardly seemed to notice as François put his arms around him and tugged at his coat, but he did let his arms fall to his sides so that the other man could pull the coat off of him.

Then, watching, François removed his own ribbon and coat, and his blouse as well, tossing everything on a chair. Jean went over and arranged the clothing neatly, though he did not hang anything in the wardrobe.

Afterward, François knelt behind the girl and began touching her, running his fingers up and down her ribs, kissing the side of her neck and pressing himself to her. Every now and then he would turn his eyes to Claude-Michel's erection, or his face, watching intently.

After several minutes, Claude-Michel took in a big breath and said, "That is enough, my dear. Save some for the finale." She looked up. He closed his mouth quickly.

François whispered in her ear, "I want to spank you."

Claude-Michel raised his eyebrows. The two men looked at each other.

The girl dropped her gaze demurely, then raised her eyes and looked at Claude-Michel mischievously before Jean caught her attention. "What about him?" she asked. "Is he going to play with us?"

"Not this time," Claude-Michel said. "I think you'll find my friend and I are as much as you can handle."

François got up and pulled her off the floor, then sat on the edge of the mattress and took her across his knee. While he watched, Claude-Michel finished undressing and sat in the chair, stroking himself periodically. François placed his hand on the girl's plump *derriere* and turned to give me a significant look. I tried to hold his gaze, but could not. I wondered what he was thinking.

The spanking François gave the girl was nothing like the one Claude-Michel had given me. He smacked her lightly at first, and then went on to sharper stings, making her cry out from time to time, then stopping to stroke her bottom. In between the harsher sessions, she wiggled on his lap and called him "*Signore.*"

When he finished, she went to her knees beside him, placing her cheek against his thigh. "Please don't punish me anymore," she teased. "I'll be a good girl."

François shot me a look over his shoulder. I looked away.

"Very, very nice," Claude-Michel said to François. "You may deserve to be promoted after such a display."

"I would like that very much," he answered. "In fact, I think, since we are a family, I should assist you in the discipline of our errant children, not just of whores."

My blood went cold. I knew he was talking about me. "Claude-Michel—"

Claude-Michel looked momentarily agitated. "I think there are better times to discuss this, François."

François gave him a forced smile. "You are right, of course," he said, with a slight bow of the head. He looked down at the girl, who looked up at him with wide eyes. She smiled.

"Things have changed a great deal," Claude-Michel said softly. "And you are right. It is the four of us." He seemed to consider his words. "Mine is the final word on all matters," he said slowly. "But you may have both sexual rights and the right of punishment over Chloe and

Jean—when I am not busy with them instead, and unless I decide to revoke this right."

François listened intently. His expression softened, as though he could not believe what he was hearing. "Thank you, Claude-Michel," he said.

I could not believe it either, but I didn't say anything because tears were threatening to come.

Claude-Michel got on his knees behind the girl and lowered himself over her body. "Let me assure you that you will not die here tonight," he said. "But you will feel pain, perhaps great fear." As he said this, his hand traveled her body. "If you are disobedient, you will be whipped with that riding crop. And this will be no game. Do you understand this?"

The smile left her face. "Why? What?"

Claude-Michel hoisted her onto the bed and flipped her over, then showed her his fangs. Her eyes widened and her lips opened for a scream, but he placed his hand over her mouth. Her eyes were very wide. "Do you know what I am?" he asked, and moved his hand.

She shook her head frantically. Tears glistened in her eyes.

"Have you ever been taken by a vampire?" he whispered.

"No," she whispered. François removed his boots.

Claude-Michel lowered his head, fluttered his eyes shut, and took in a deep breath. "You smell lovely," he said. "I am so hungry." With that he held down her flailing body and pressed his fangs into her throat. The sharp smell of blood hit me full in the face. François tugged his blouse over his head and threw himself at the girl, trying to find a way to puncture her throat even as Claude-Michel fed, but there was not enough room. The girl tried to fight them off, but managed only to buck beneath Claude-

Michel. Seeing Claude-Michel force his will on her sent such a surge through my body that I wanted to be the one under him. In that moment I wished he had been my maker instead of the other way around.

Claude-Michel looked up at François. "I have fed since you," he said, and got up. François opened his breeches and mounted her eagerly, drawing from the wounds and grinding his crotch into hers simultaneously, through the fabric.

My eyes widened like saucers when Claude-Michel stood behind François and slid his friend's breeches down his slender hips, then grasped the shaft of François's erection. François gasped, blowing a bubble in the girl's blood before resealing the wound with his lips. Claude-Michel guided François's erection into the girl, in spite of her panicked undulations, and François pounded into her relentlessly.

It wasn't long before François raised his head and cried out. The girl had grown quiet, and simply stared at them with wide eyes. François rolled off her and lay on the bed as Claude-Michel grinned at him. Then Claude-Michel took his turn, piercing her again with his fangs and penetrating her with his erection as François watched sleepily. She whimpered quietly and tried to move against him. François and Claude-Michel looked into each other's eyes with the tenderness of lovers.

Chapter Thirteen

IN THE hours before dawn, Claude-Michel had Jean pack our things, and supervised as François and I wrestled the groggy prostitute into my extra dress. They arranged her on the bed in a position resembling repose, but she groaned and tried to turn over.

"Tie a cravat around those bites," he said. "Loosen her clothing, too. The landlord knows what she was here for."

Jean stood by the bed, inspecting the riding crop Claude-Michel had come in with as though mesmerized.

"Jean!" Claude-Michel said sharply, looking satisfied when the poor boy jumped. "Stop daydreaming and get to work."

"*Oui, Monsieur,*" Jean replied, and put the crop away hastily.

"Where will we go?" I asked Claude-Michel. "It was difficult to find this place."

"I do not know," he said irritably. "But we cannot remain here. The girl will talk. And she has marks."

"Perhaps you should have thought of that before," I said.

He grabbed my arm and whirled me around to face him. I looked him in the eye and would not back down. At that moment, I did not care about punishment.

"Someone is jealous," François sing-songed, and sat on the bed near the girl, his hands behind his head.

I wanted so badly to tell François what I thought, but my courage was short-lived. I was relieved when Claude-Michel let me go to call Jean over to give him money. "Pay the landlord for an extra day. Do not tell him we are leaving for good. And buy wine, bread and cheese for yourself and the girl."

"Yes, *Monsieur*," he said, and hurried away.

"Who do you think she is jealous of, Claude-Michel— you or me?" François asked.

"Shut up, François," Claude-Michel said, and went to the window. "I have to think."

"But of course," François replied, and closed his eyes.

I sat on the couch with my arms crossed. So far the day had started terribly. Within moments, however, Jean burst into the room with promising news.

"*Messieurs*, there is something you should know about. A man downstairs needs guards for his carriage to protect his sister."

Claude-Michel, who had moved away from the window in favor of pacing, looked up. Then he hurried out the door. I had to follow—so, of course, François wasn't far behind.

Downstairs, we could not help but hear their conversation. There were two men, perhaps a little older than I, sitting near the cold fireplace.

"But I can't take my sister across the country with no protection!" the youngest of the two said. He looked like a rosy-cheeked cherub. "What of bandits?"

"You can't allow her to miss her own wedding either," his friend said sympathetically. "Anyway, what happened to those men you hired?"

"They got a better offer somewhere else. There is the irony of hiring men—those vulgar enough to protect one from criminals are often no better than criminals themselves."

"I don't see that you have a choice, Bernardo. It would disgrace your entire family—and you especially, since you insisted on bringing your sister here in the first place."

"It was for her health. She is allergic to the Northern air."

"Of course, of course. But tell me...how did you manage that trip?"

"Our uncle arranged it. I only came as a companion for my sister," Bernardo said with a sigh. "I'm simply no good in business dealings."

Claude-Michel approached them, smiling. "Excuse me, young man. I couldn't help but overhear your predicament. Where did you say your sister's wedding was to be held?"

The young man—a cherub with plump, pink cheeks and light brown curls—gave him a haughty look. "I did not say, sir. What business would a Frenchman have in my affairs?"

"I don't mean to pry," Claude-Michel said with a regal nod of his head. "But you seem in need of protection of a more gentlemanly sort than you had. My friend Monsieur Villaforte and I are masters of both sword and pistol, and we are far from being ruffians. We are also in need of transportation to Venice. You are in need of protection. I simply thought we could reach an agreement."

"See?" the friend said. "Ask and you shall receive."

"How do I know you won't rob me?" the young man asked.

"Le Compte Louis Claude-Michel du Fresne does not rob people, young *Monsieur*. Are you lodging here?"

"Yes, but—"

"Good. Pack your things. My companions and I are ready to leave."

The cherub gave his friend a worried look.

"Go on," the friend said. "You can't pass up an opportunity like this one. These men are obviously gentlemen. You don't often find gentlemen willing to hire themselves out."

"No," Bernardo said. "It makes me wonder what strange circumstance led them to it."

"You've no other choice," the friend said. "Except to travel unaccompanied."

"That would not be wise," Claude-Michel said. "Especially, if you don't mind my saying, when one has a maiden in tow. There are dangerous men about."

"Yes," Bernardo said. "I worry for my sister's safety." His gaze shifted to me. "Your wife will perhaps provide company for my sister," he said.

"Wife?" Claude-Michel said, then caught himself. "Oh yes. Of course," he said. "She is quite the conversationalist. If you will show my men to your carriage, my wife and I will settle our business with the landlord."

François glared at him for that, but went with Bernardo and his friend. I followed Claude-Michel to the bar. Claude-Michel explained to the innkeeper that they had taxed the prostitute's abilities so much, he thought it best she be allowed to sleep it off for the day.

The innkeeper looked at me, confused, no doubt wondering why a man would bring a prostitute into his room with his wife present. "For my friend," he explained.

"Most are not so generous with whores, *Signore*, no matter what they've done with them. Or to friends."

"Then I am a rare man, my friend, the likes of which you shall never meet again. *Buon giorno*."

* * * *

Bernardo's young sister, whose name was Florentine, had the same rosy cheeks, with golden hair and eyes the color of turquoise from the New World. She was already in the carriage by the time we came, sitting in the forward-facing seat. Claude-Michel bowed in greeting. Florentine smiled and lowered her eyes before meeting his again, more boldly this time. I could tell she was strongly attracted to him, but I was too put out by the night before to care.

"At your service, *cherie*," he said with a bow.

Bernardo didn't have a driver, so Jean climbed into the driver's seat. It was a large carriage, with an extra forward-facing seat behind Florentine's where two more passengers could sit side-by side, or one person could stretch out. Claude-Michel suggested I take it first, as I "no doubt got little rest the night before."

I took it, but I did not lie down right away. I sat behind Bernardo at the end opposite to Florentine and Claude-Michel, where I could see them better. When I climbed in, I looked at Florentine from head to toe as I passed. She smiled up at me, pretending to be friendly. At that moment, I wanted to slap her face, but not as much as I wanted to slap Claude-Michel's for the amused smile he gave me.

François, I wanted to kill. He snickered audibly and took the place next to Claude-Michel.

Once everyone had settled, Claude-Michel began asking about Florentine's wedding and found she was betrothed to a man who was "rather old."

"Florentine!" her brother admonished. "He is a very wealthy man, and a good friend of Papa's. And he has always treated you well. Remember the doll he gave you that you adored?"

"I was eight years old, Bernardo. And he was thirty-two. I do like him, but—"

"You agreed he would make a good husband," Bernardo said.

"I'll be *bored*, Bernardo."

"You won't be bored. He'll take you to the theatre."

She sighed heavily and stared out the window.

Bernardo looked at Claude-Michel nervously. "You have to excuse my sister, *Signore*. She has such romantic notions."

"But romance is the great adventure of life," Claude-Michel said, with a long look at Florentine. She stole a glance at him out of the corner of her eye. Even from here I could see her pretending to restrain her smile.

We camped in the forest in late afternoon. Jean built a fire and took care of the horses, while Claude-Michel went into the forest to relieve himself. I wondered if he really needed to, since vampires do that far less than regular people, especially when blood is scarce.

I decided to follow him. "I need to speak with you. Claude-Michel," I said.

"Then speak," he answered without stopping.

At first I stopped, unable to believe his continued arrogance. Then I caught up with him and blocked his way. "Claude-Michel. I don't understand you. One day you beat me. The next you woo me, then you give François rights with me. Now you won't even speak to me."

He stopped and regarded me sternly. "It is, my lovely pet, because of your childish insistence that I conduct my affairs differently. You will accept my attentions as I choose to give them. You will accept punishment when it comes, and—yes—you will obey François as well. I grow tired of your childishness. Angelique accepted my habits, and you will do the same."

The comparison to his wife felt like a slap. I looked away momentarily. My lips went slack. I blinked back tears. "Claude-Michel...you can't give him rights over me."

"I can," he said. "And I must. François needs something to occupy him or he becomes impossible."

"Yes," François said from behind Claude-Michel, examining his fingernails. "He does. Especially when he has his hair pulled and is shown blatant disrespect."

Claude-Michel did not seem surprised at François' sudden appearance. I suspected he had known he was there all along. But at his words, Claude-Michel furrowed his brow at me. I could not stop myself from giving him a horrified look.

"What is this?" Claude-Michel asked. "What is he talking about, Chloe?"

François kept his eyes on me as he approached. "Yesterday evening, while I was getting ready to go out, she pulled my hair and spoke to me in a very threatening manner. She demanded submission because she turned us into what we are."

Claude-Michel considered François's words. Anger darkened his eyes and made me afraid. "Is this true, Chloe?"

I fought to control my expressions, but I knew he could see the panic inside of me. Even though I knew it was a stupid thing to do, I gave François a beseeching look, but he answered it with one of blissful ignorance. It seemed grotesque in the forest.

I nodded and lowered my eyes. "Yes."

"Would you do such a thing with me?" Claude-Michel asked in low tones.

I shook my head frantically and approached him. "No, Claude-Michel, I would never—"

"Then why would you do it to my oldest friend?"

I stopped, not daring to touch him. My lip trembled. "I—" I began, but did not continue.

"And now he has the right to punish you for it."

A tear escaped my eye, but I ignored it. "Please, Claude-Michel—"

"I want to hear nothing more from you about this," Claude-Michel said with a wave of his hand. "François, why did you not tell me sooner?"

"I understood she was upset, and at the time wished to make light of it. But as time wears on, the roles you and I both play become more and more clear as the elder members of our family." He emphasized the last word. "For Chloe's sake, I should give her the benefit of my guidance...only in addition to yours, of course."

Claude-Michel smiled. "And for François' sake as well?" he said.

François gave him the same look of wide-eyed innocence. It chilled me to the bone.

"Were we alone, François," he said evenly, "I would instruct you to give Chloe the benefit of your guidance this moment, as I watched. At the moment, however, it is not wise to alarm our hosts. When we have grown to know them better, we will make an example of Chloe."

I panicked. "What are you saying?" I asked, but a look from Claude-Michel silenced me.

François turned to Claude-Michel with raised eyebrows. "Grown to know them better, Claude-Michel?"

"But of course, François. You cannot allow such an opportunity to pass. We are in need of a more permanent food supply. We cannot live from prostitutes forever. And they are such a lovely pair."

"Take them...by seduction or by force?" François asked.

He turned to me. "It is possible, yes?" he asked. "The bite of the vampire has intoxicating effects?"

I nodded. "The bite made most of Gunnar's crew docile. Gunnar fed from each of them on a regular basis. To keep them loyal, he said."

"So you see," Claude-Michel said to François. "We can win their cooperation by feasting."

"And if the bite doesn't quite have that effect?" François asked.

"Then we keep them by force," Claude-Michel answered.

Chapter Fourteen

SINCE CLAUDE-MICHEL'S plan involved me seducing Bernardo, I sat beside him in the carriage the following morning and suggested Florentine stretch out on the extra seat behind the men.

"It is very comfortable," I lied.

François gave me a self-satisfied look and inched closer to Claude-Michel. I raised my chin at him to show I didn't care, and turned to Bernardo. I knew Claude-Michel watched the whole thing for his own amusement, but I wondered exactly what amused him so—François' obvious play for his romantic affections, or my reluctant acquiescence to his wishes in the face of certain punishment. Perhaps it was Bernardo's squirming.

I periodically touched Bernardo's thigh or a lock of his hair, pretending to do so absently. He eyed Claude-Michel as though expecting him to run him through on the spot. Later that day, when we stopped to rest the horses and stretch our legs, Claude-Michel pulled the boy aside. I thought Bernardo would wet his breeches. "Please humor my wife," I heard him say. "She becomes intolerable if she doesn't have the opportunity to practice her charms."

"Oh," Bernardo said. "I will try."

After that, he relaxed a little and began to open up, even telling a story. Florentine refused to sit in the back, instead insisting on sitting on the other side of her brother, across from Claude-Michel. She became flirtatious and happy, except when the wedding was mentioned.

"How old is this ancient man?" Claude-Michel asked.

"Forty," the girl said with a pout. I put a hand over my mouth, but couldn't stifle a laugh as both Claude-Michel and François' smiles froze momentarily on their faces. Florentine noticed as well, and spoke quickly. "But he is not like you. You are much more handsome than he is," she said, leaning forward and looking from Claude-Michel to François. "And there is something about you that makes you seem so alive, so virile."

"Florentine!"

"It's only a word, Bernardo," she said crossly. "It isn't a sin to compliment our guests, is it?"

"They are not our guests," Bernardo whispered between clenched teeth. "They are men hired to protect us."

"They're counts," she said. "And we didn't hire them. You'll have to forgive my brother," she said. "He's a prude."

That was fodder I couldn't pass up. "Is he?" I purred.

Bernardo glowered, ignoring my fingers playing in his hair.

"You're very beautiful," Florentine said to me suddenly.

I looked up. The earnestness in the girl's wide, blue eyes made my chest tighten. When Florentine gave me a hesitant smile, I willed my lips not to move. I did not want to like her. I knew what was in store for her and I could not afford to feel pity. We needed food too badly.

"Thank you," I said, and turned back to Bernardo. "See?" I said, pouting on purpose. "Your *sister* likes me." At that, he seemed to relax a little.

"She is right," Bernardo said. "You are beautiful. You are a very lucky man, *Signore* du Fresne."

"Yes," Claude-Michel said. "Beautiful and talented." He looked at me with approval, which made me feel warm, even though I knew he was doing it for Bernardo's benefit.

When it was time to stop for the evening, Bernardo excused himself and went into the woods. Claude-Michel gave me an urgent look, so I followed him while François distracted Florentine with a bat he had spotted.

I moved easily among the dark trees, vaguely aware of the beauty in the shadows. Tonight, we had stopped later than we had the night before and so the forest floor was darker—black to the eyes of any regular human. But my eyes detected layer upon layer of darkness, each existing in its own plane. The crescent moon caused the trees to cast a veiny network over everything, so that the forest appeared to be a whispering, organic net. Shapes slithered and darted through the trees. I could hear the rustling of creatures in their burrows, and the wet, rhythmic sounds of human organs jostling just ahead. Those were the sounds that drew me on, as the urge to chase became a living thing within me. Bernardo's warm, yeasty smell became pungent. We were linked as quarry and hunter. I was marked, just as he was, unable to escape the fate that Gunnar had chosen for me. I remembered the last time I had run through a forest, and felt glad I was now the one who pursued.

Habit made me pull my tongue back into my mouth as my fangs grew. My stomach growled and the spot between my legs stung with an excitement I had not known before the change. And then I saw him.

He stood with his back to me, pumping his organ furiously with frantic little pants. Silent as the shadows, I crept up behind him and clapped a hand over his mouth.

"Bernardo," I purred, as Claude-Michel had purred my name.

For a moment, he stood still. I thought he might try to break from my grasp, but he did not move, not even to let go of his erection. I slid my free hand beneath the fabric of his shirt, running the palm over his soft belly, and pulled him tightly against me. He was no taller than I. Reaching a vein wouldn't be difficult, but I knew Claude-Michel would not be pleased if he were not the one to master the boy.

"You may scream if you like," I said, and removed my hand from his mouth to slide it into his breeches and find the smooth flesh of his *derriere*. He drew in a violent breath.

"*Signora* du Fresne," he whispered. "What are you doing here? Where is your husband?"

"He is occupied. I wished to speak with you...in private."

His hand trembled, but began to move slowly along the shaft. "I have to go back. My sister needs me."

"*I* need you," I said. "Have you ever been pleasured by a woman?"

"Yes," he said, somewhat indignantly.

"Not one like me," I said, and made him turn around. Crouching in front of him, I took his hand away and slipped my mouth around the slick head of his cock, which stiffened even more.

"But your husband, *Signora*—"

"He cares nothing for my body, only my money," I said, pumping the base of his member as Gunnar had shown me. "He doesn't care what I do."

The boy moaned and fell back against the tree as I worked with my hand and mouth to bring him close to climax, then shifted my attention to the tight little sac between his legs. There were footsteps in the woods I knew only I could hear. When I saw Claude-Michel watching from the shadows among the trees, I drew Bernardo's breeches down to his ankles and lay back on the leaves. He gave up his resistance then and eagerly pulled up my skirts, giving me a brief look of surprise when he discovered there was nothing under them.

"*Signora*," he said in the same tone he'd used to admonish his sister. Then he pushed into me with a groan of intense pleasure and began to thrust. In a moment, Claude-Michel had him, with a hand clamped over his mouth. Bernardo's eyes grew wide. He froze.

"What are you doing with my wife, eh?" Claude-Michel whispered in silky tones. Bernardo whimpered. I could feel him soften inside me. "Shh," Claude-Michel said. "Don't answer. It is not your fault. You don't know what she is."

I waited for waves of disgust to wash over me, but they did not come. In spite of my anger at Claude-Michel for being such an unrepentant libertine, I felt intrigued by watching him take control of the boy, and enjoyed the sensation of the boy's trembling atop my belly and against my bare inner thighs. I saw by the way Claude-Michel held his mouth that his teeth had grown also. He pursed his lips around his fangs, an expression I found excruciatingly beautiful on his face. Bernardo's entire body went limp.

"You have such a lovely sister," Claude-Michel purred. "François and I could do such things to her."

From somewhere deep inside the young man, an enraged scream formed, forcing its way up through his throat, only to die against Claude-Michel's unyielding hand. It made me want to beg Claude-Michel to fuck me right there on the ground. Bernardo tried to fight his way free, but could not move his captor.

"Shh," Claude-Michel said. "If you are silent, we will not harm your sister. But if you scream, we could do such things." The boy held still, breathing heavily, casting his eyes about wildly in the darkness. "Your sister is alone with François and Jean," Claude-Michel said. "If they hear your screams they will have their way with her. Do I have your word?"

Bernardo nodded.

"Very nice," Claude-Michel said, and let go of his mouth. Bernardo hung his head like a winded animal, panting.

I reached up to soothe his head with my fingers in his curls. He jumped as though he'd forgotten I was there. "There now," I said. "It will be all right."

"What do you want?" he whispered.

"It's all right," I repeated. "I'm here." Behind him, Claude-Michel was unfastening his own breeches. It occurs to me now that I should have been horrified. But I wasn't. I wanted to see Claude-Michel take this frightened young man.

"A man of breeding learns that there are many pleasures in life," Claude-Michel said. "Beautiful women are one of our greatest joys. But one can not forget the pleasure young men discover together, and the sight of a beautiful boy never fails to stir the old longings."

"Please," Bernardo whispered. "Don't do this." He blinked rapidly. His eyes filled with tears.

"Surely you have been taken by a man before," Claude-Michel whispered.

"Never," Bernardo said. His tone was defiant, but I could hear a sob welling up in his throat.

Claude-Michel, now looming in the darkness behind him, smiled. "The pleasure of deflowering a virgin," he said. "This is an exquisite thing."

"Please," Bernardo said frantically, trying to twist around to see Claude-Michel, though it was almost completely dark now.

Claude-Michel grasped the young man's hips and pressed against him with the head of his erection. "Remember," he said. "If you scream, your sister will suffer the same fate."

Impulsively, I grabbed the boy's head and covered his mouth with mine as Claude-Michel pressed into him. Bernardo bucked and struggled wildly but we held him tightly between us. When his erection returned, Claude-Michel encircled him around the abdomen with one arm and ordered him to enter me again.

"You're killing me," he gasped.

"Do it," Claude-Michel growled. Bernardo obeyed with trembling hands, and Claude-Michel supported his own weight on his palms as he ground his hips into him. I gasped and held Bernardo tightly. Claude-Michel's hair curled just a little, beautifully, against his cheeks. Finally, Bernardo widened his eyes and gasped. I felt his hips give a few little thrusts before he collapsed on top of me as Claude-Michel growled with the force of his own climax.

"Now you have been taken by a man," Claude-Michel whispered, raising himself to his knees and using his handkerchief to clean himself before closing his breeches. "Or more than a man."

Bernardo began to cry against me. I was thankful he could not see my fangs in the darkness. Finally, Claude-Michel pulled him off of me and pinned him to the ground with a self-satisfied smile. "Do you know what I am?" he asked, taking no pains to hide his fangs. It was dark enough, I knew, for the boy to assume his eyes were playing tricks on him if he saw them now.

"You're a bastard and a sodomite," Bernardo said without conviction.

"Yes," Claude-Michel said. "True. But I am something else as well." He nosed around the collar of Bernardo's blouse. "Remember your promise not to scream," he said. "Remember your sister." And with that he plunged his fangs deep into the boy's throat.

I watched Bernardo struggle. I knew it was not his will alone that allowed him to fight so hard. This time, in the jaws of a predator who wanted his blood, he instinctively drew upon the will of his distant ancestors, perhaps reliving the last memories of some. He cried out, but the sound he made was not a scream, nor did it sound like any human utterance I had ever heard. It was similar to the keening of a dying rabbit, primal and haunting.

Before long, the struggling stopped, and the boy lay docile on the forest floor as Claude-Michel drank his fill.

* * * *

I followed Claude-Michel as he carried the dazed boy back to our camp like a weakened damsel in his arms. I forced myself to look at Florentine as she spied her brother. Her forehead wrinkled and she cried out, trying to jump up to go to him. François, sitting next to her on a blanket, grabbed her arm.

"It looks like he was bitten," François said softly into her ear. "He will be fine in a day or two."

"Bitten?" she asked, her tone rising in pitch. She remained on her knees, in spite of François's restraining hold on her arm. On her other side, Jean rose into a crouch and turned toward her as if to block her path.

"Floren—" the boy gasped, reaching for her as Claude-Michel carried him past.

"Bernardo?" she called, now straining against François and Jean, who grabbed her upper arms. For a moment the determined look on Jean's face caught me by surprise, and I thought the young man who fell to his knees before Claude-Michel at a moment's notice might ravish the girl himself. "What's wrong, Bernardo?" she called helplessly.

"Vam—" was all Bernardo could manage before Claude-Michel got him into the carriage.

I went to the girl, who had stopped struggling against François and Jean, but who still stared pitifully in the direction of the carriage. Claude-Michel emerged with a look of lecherous triumph on his face. Jean stepped aside as his master approached.

"You will be all right," I said gently, and maybe foolishly. "You won't die. I promise you won't die."

Florentine turned to me with a pained look on her face and streaming tears. "Die?" she said. "What? What's wrong with Bernardo?" she almost screamed.

François held her tighter and pressed his cheek against her ear. "Shh," he said. "No screaming."

Claude-Michel crouched in front of her and lightly stroked her cheek. She watched his hands like a frightened animal, periodically trying to pull away, but managing only to press against François. "Your brother is sleeping," Claude-Michel said. "He will wake up tomorrow."

Florentine looked up at Claude-Michel. He reached around and began to unfasten her hairpins. Her flushed cheeks made her look like a child. "What are you doing?" she asked, but no longer tried to escape.

"Do you know what I am?" he cooed.

A confused expression came over her face.

"Do you know what I am?" he repeated, smiling carelessly. She shook her head slowly and watched him warily. He lowered his mouth to her ear and whispered, "Vampire."

Her eyes widened, and she shook her head again, frantically this time. "No," she said, and tried to wrench her body out of François' grasp.

"We are all vampires," he said. "Except for Jean, who has been providing most of our meals. He needs a rest."

Her gaze flicked from Claude-Michel to me to Jean and back to Claude-Michel. Then she tried again to get away, straining toward the carriage. "Bernardo!" she called. "Bernardo!" But her brother did not answer.

Claude-Michel turned her face roughly toward him. "We are hungry," he said. "And our loins are on fire."

When François let go of her arms and reached around to untie the lace of her bodice, she tried to bolt toward the carriage. Claude-Michel grabbed her upper arms and shook her. "Would you open your virgin flower to a mere mortal?"

"But my wedding—"

"Will take place on this forest floor," he said. "With me."

Those words had such an effect on her. She did not struggle as he and François undressed her and lay out the dress on the ground so she would have something to lie upon. I went to her and pet her hair as he touched and kissed her, and let her see his fangs. I smiled carefully, because I was quickly learning to become aroused whenever I saw Claude-Michel take some poor, innocent creature.

Jean sat nearby, watching with interest, turning a stone over and over in the fingers of one hand. François got up and stretched, glancing back at them from time to time, finally standing with his back against a tree, arms crossed, watching me. I shivered as I thought about what was to happen to me at his hands, but pushed the images out of my mind and focused my attention on what was happening to Florentine.

As Claude-Michel kissed her small, creamy breasts, she turned her turquoise eyes up to me. I smiled, to put her at ease. "It will be all right," I whispered, as much for my own benefit as for hers. "This is necessary."

She nodded and closed her eyes, gasping from time to time as Claude-Michel's fangs grazed her skin, or as his tongue lapped at a particularly sensitive part of her body.

He was much gentler with Florentine than he had been with Bernardo, perhaps because he knew she wanted him. Perhaps because she was a virgin. He teased the soft folds between her legs with the tip of his tongue. She took in breath like a corpse reanimated. Her eyes popped open. For a moment, I thought she would try to get up, but she only looked at me. I bent down and kissed her forehead.

"Let yourself enjoy it," I whispered.

Claude-Michel suddenly raised himself on his knees and removed his blouse, smiling down at her, letting her see him. When he freed his erection, I could tell by the way her face crumpled she had never seen a man's nude crotch before. She whimpered.

Claude-Michel positioned himself at her opening and gently shushed her. It didn't take him long to get it in. Florentine yelped when he filled her, but he settled on top of her body and began to whisper as he worked his hips slowly, getting her used to the sensation, letting her find her pleasure. He kissed away her tears and called her beautiful. I watched him pumping her for many minutes, growing aroused myself, and wondering if I could tempt him in my direction when he was finished making feeders.

Finally, he lowered his head and began to nuzzle her neck. All at once, she realized what he was doing and began to lose her nerve. "No," she whined. "Please."

But it was too late. Her eyes widened and she gasped and I knew he had pierced her. Her struggles ceased and her eyes glazed over as Bernardo's had, as Claude-Michel took her blood.

Chapter Fifteen

CLAUDE-MICHEL PROMISED to be mine the very next night, but it was his turn to guard us as we slept. I, however, couldn't sleep, though I tried very hard, in Jean's arms on the floor of the carriage. François napped on the bench above us. I could tell he was aware of me, watching me somehow.

After Jean started snoring, I whispered to François, "Why do you hate me so much?"

"My dear, I don't hate you," he said without opening his eyes. "I simply want you firmly in your place."

I turned my body toward him.

He sat up, propping his back against the side of the carriage, and glanced out the window at Claude-Michel. François almost smiled and turned lazily back to me. "Claude-Michel and I have known each other all of our lives, and I have adored him every minute. We did everything together, and of course I was much too young to know what my feelings meant. I didn't know until later, and then I stupidly waited around for him to take me. He took other boys, why not me? Then he was married, and by then, I had fallen into a habit. There was a certain way we existed and I thought then, that if I changed any little thing, the whole universe we'd created would destroy itself."

The intensity in his eyes frightened me.

"Now the one person who stood between us is gone, and you are not going to take her place."

I narrowed my eyes at him, determined not to show my fear.

"I have stood beside Claude-Michel longer than you have been alive," François said. "I have shared everything with him. I was with him in the war, and I saved him from that Katarina woman."

That was a name that interested me, because I had heard Claude-Michel speaking to Francois about finding her. "Saved him? How?"

"We were due back in Paris and he wasn't going to leave. So I tipped off the local constable, told him where the camp was. Added that a few of the men were forming a plot to kidnap and rape one of the city's high-placed young ladies."

"They were?"

"Oh I don't know," he said with a flourish of his hand. "Probably. It doesn't matter. The camp was raided. I thought there would be beatings perhaps. But the Gypsies fought them and the father was killed."

"Katarina's?"

François nodded. Something in his face changed and I could see he felt regret. "Claude-Michel had learned to love the violin while listening to that man play. So Katarina returned and put her father's violin in our room as he slept. I was awake. She told me to tell him, so I did. Of course, the next day, he struck me for not waking him. He wanted to go and find her, but it was too late."

"That is a terrible thing to do, telling the constable such a thing. It sounds like Claude-Michel loved her."

"That woman was almost forty years old, and a Gypsy. What would he have done? He was twenty, with a life at court, in Paris, awaiting him. I saved him."

"Does he know?"

"Perhaps." For a while François was silent. "That was the violin your pirate destroyed. His beloved Gypsy violin. The last vestige of that hopeless dream of Katarina. Or so I thought. Now he insists on tracking down that woman's son. I am not going to let a dead woman or her bastard child stand between us," he said.

Son? I wanted to say. It was news to me.

"Or you," he said with a sneer, swinging his legs off the side of the bench. "And now I'd better wake our guard before the wolves get us all." He climbed down into the floor and straddled me on all fours. "Not one word of this to him. Understand...*cherie?*"

"I understand," I said.

He cupped my breast through my blouse.

"What are you doing?" I asked. "You don't even like women."

He tweaked my nipple painfully, trying to make me flinch. As he spoke he ran his hand down my stomach, and my leg, pulling up my gown. "Let's just say I've learned a certain appreciation over the years. Claude-Michel has taken you, so when I take you, it will be close to making love with him. You will be one more thing that ties us together, like a favorite game. Or a toy."

I gaped at him as his fingers found their way inside of me. He kept his eyes on me as he worked them in and out, stimulating my clit with his thumb, awakening my body. I didn't expect what happened next, didn't expect him to open his breeches and tease me with the head of his erection.

"What are you doing, François?" I hissed at him.

"What Claude-Michel gave me the right to do," he said, and pushed the length of his erection into me. I couldn't help but gasp. Then I looked at Jean. He opened his eyes briefly, registered what was happening, and turned his back on us.

My body betrayed me, just as it always had with Gunnar. I was tired of fighting it, so I raised my hips to meet his. If this was to be my place in their little "family," then I would enjoy what pleasure there was as a result, just as I had advised Florentine to do. Becoming more excited, François lowered his head into my hair and warmed my neck with his whispers.

"Do you remember the story he told you on the ship? Of spanking his wife?"

"Yes," I whispered back. The sound of his voice in my ear lulled me into his rhythm. "But you were delirious with fever."

"Not so delirious that I was not aware the two of you talked. I remember that night well. And Claude-Michel did not tell you what he was doing before he discovered his son had not come to the palace."

François paused to breathe in my ear while thrusting into me. My lips parted and I breathed with him as his body moved against mine. I could not believe this was happening, could not believe how excited I had become by François' rutting into me on the floor of Bernardo's carriage.

"He was chasing his newest conquest through the king's labyrinth. And I was chasing both of them." He groaned with the memory and slowed his pace, pushing into me and grinding. "There were many lovers in the labyrinth that night, and Claude-Michel had to pardon himself many times. The girl was a young *marquese*, newly married. When he caught her, I was on the other side of the hedge, well out of view. I heard her squeal, and it made me desperate to see through the hedge, so I made a small hole with my hand. I saw him holding her against him, pressing her stomach through her corset, and feeling through the layers of her skirts. The night...smelled like horses and sweat.

"I had to force myself to breathe quietly while I touched myself, but I was so excited by the sounds of their passion, and to hear her pretend to struggle against him."

"Did you take out your erection?" I asked. His story had excited me too much to resist.

"Yes. It was hard and dripping. I wanted to fuck that girl with Claude-Michel. I wanted to fuck her as he fucked me at the same time. I was sure, at least, that I would have her later, when he grew tired of her."

His words troubled me for a moment, but I refused to think of Claude-Michel losing interest, especially after he had said he wanted to keep me, as he had kept his wife and Jean.

"She complained that he would ruin her wig, and whined about some promise he had made to play his violin for her, that the queen found it most enchanting. It was true. But he was not interested in violins. He wanted to take this girl, right there in the hedges. Just as I am taking you now," he added, lowering his voice dangerously.

It was my turn to groan.

"'I have other talents, *Madame*, that I would prefer to demonstrate,' is what he told her, and pulled her skirt up over her thighs. I gasped with her as Claude-Michel put his fingers inside of her. He whispered, but I could still hear what he said. 'Don't make me come for you in the small hours, *cherie*, when no one is awake to help you.'"

For a moment, François simply rocked his hips against me and I raised mine to meet his. My hip rubbed against Jean's *derriere* with our fucking, but he did not move to get away from it.

"She asked him why," François whispered. "'Because then, my dear, I will have no mercy. You will wake to find me in your bed, my eyes wild with desire.' Of course," François breathed, "I knew those words well enough to whisper them as he whispered them. 'I will keep you from crying out, like this...'"

François put his hand over my mouth.

"Do you know what I will do to you then? Hmm?"

He looked at me so intently, I wondered if the story had lapsed into the present. I wondered if the words were now for me. I simply stared at him, my worry igniting my desire even more.

François spoke between clenched teeth. "'I will take you without mercy, like an animal. I will be a growling, snarling thing, and you will be helpless beneath me.' When I heard him say that, I spilled my pearls into the hedge."

He gave me a self-satisfied look as his body claimed mine, but I did not care. His thrusting and his breathing grew more insistent. Finally, he lowered his face into my hair and breathed Claude-Michel's name, increasing the force of his thrusting until he made me whimper, emptying himself into me.

He stayed where he was for many moments, composing himself, gaining control of his breathing. Then, suddenly, he raised himself on his knees and fastened his breeches. "I wish to be with Claude-Michel alone," he said. "Don't disturb us."

I nodded. When he had gone, I lay there and pleasured myself while listening to them, until an orgasm warmed my belly and spread down my legs with tendrils of fire.

They spoke softly, but perhaps they had forgotten about vampire hearing, because I understood all they said without difficulty. "Did you enjoy yourself this evening, *mon ami*?" François asked.

"It was extraordinary," Claude-Michel said. "The brother and sister are quite a pair."

I pulled myself away from Jean and opened the curtain so that I could see Claude-Michel and François, then took François's old place on the seat, leaning against the carriage wall. Their voices came to me softly but clearly.

"Good," François said. "I am glad you enjoyed it."

François reached out and fondled a curl near Claude-Michel's jaw. "You need grooming," he said.

"Yes," Claude-Michel replied.

I felt a strange feeling—separate, knowing that the two men shared something I could never penetrate. It saddened me.

For a while neither of them spoke. Then Claude-Michel broke the silence. "You know, François, you have been with me longer than anyone. You have been beside me through everything."

"I have to make myself feel superior somehow," François said.

Claude-Michel ignored the comment. "So much time has passed without my notice. Now that everything has come to an abrupt halt..." Claude-Michel sighed. I wondered if he was talking about the wedding plans he had been making for his son. Then he continued. "Do you remember when we were boys and—" He stopped suddenly. "I am still cutting myself on these damned fangs."

François leaned over and kissed him, right on the mouth. I wanted to run out there and pull his "golden locks" out by the roots. "I have loved you longer than you can imagine," he said.

Claude-Michel sighed. "I am not a man who speaks of love, François."

"I know."

The two sat in silence, while I sat in the carriage with my heart beating madly. I didn't hear them say anything else for a long time. I must have dozed. The next thing I knew, the sun was rising, and Claude-Michel was standing.

"They have slept long enough," he said, and looked down at François, who was still sitting with his back against the tree. "You want your consummation with Chloe, yes?" Claude-Michel asked.

It felt as though my heart stopped. I did not like the sound of that.

"My...consummation?"

"The punishment for pulling your hair. It means something to you."

My mouth went dry. I had hoped, just a little, that they would forget.

François stood. "It means you and I are the parents of this family," he said.

"And what is Chloe?"

"Less than I."

I felt my lips part. I felt as though I should be angered by those words, but they only made me sink into myself. I felt hopeless.

Claude-Michel seemed to consider this. Then he nodded once and banged on the carriage door. "Jean!" he called, and came in, nearly stepping on the boy. I did not try to hide the fact that I had been watching them. Claude-Michel seemed not to notice. François stared at me smugly.

Jean raised his head, blinking. "Both of you," Claude-Michel said, glancing at me. "Get them out here."

I gave Jean a worried look. He nodded at Claude-Michel and got up. "*Oui, Monsieur*," he said and pulled on his pants and blouse, sliding out to climb into the back. I sat where I was, looking from Claude-Michel to François. François looked at me with a mixture of disdain and pleasure.

Within moments, Jean had the others up and sitting on a blanket near the still-smoking embers. They were still groggy from their first bites. I crept out of the carriage without my bodice, but remained standing with one hand on the open door. I felt as though I may throw up at any moment. I couldn't believe this was happening, that Claude-Michel was going to let François whip me.

Florentine looked around with wide, panicked eyes. When she saw Claude-Michel, she whimpered and tried to scurry away. Jean crouched beside her and put his arm around her thin shoulders. "Shh," he said. "Shh. No one is going to hurt you today."

"Unless she doesn't do what she's told," Claude-Michel said.

Bernardo blinked up at him. "What? You—" He looked confused. His eyes widened.

Florentine's expression crumbled and she tried to squirm out of Jean's grasp. Claude-Michel squatted in front of her and touched her beneath the chin. "Did you sleep well?"

"Keep your hands off my sister," Bernardo said.

I watched all of this in horror, knowing I was to be the main attraction of this drama.

Claude-Michel turned to Bernardo and said nothing. Bernardo began to sweat. Claude-Michel gave the boy's cheek a couple of light smacks. "You don't have to be the hero who protects the virtuous woman, Bernardo. There is no longer virtue there to protect."

Bernardo looked at Florentine, who bowed her head and began to sob. There was a part of me that felt bad for them, for being babes in the woods. They had just experienced what I had experienced so many months ago, having their world torn from them and becoming slaves of another. But my pity was short-lived, even as I listened to what Claude-Michel had to say.

"Yesterday, your virgin sister was ravished by two vampires on the forest floor. You and she now belong to those vampires, and you will do what you're told or suffer the consequences."

Bernardo looked down, then reached up to touch the bite-mark on his neck. He flinched. His eyes grew larger. "What do you want?"

Claude-Michel smiled. "Your blood and your bodies."

Bernardo seemed to consider this. "What consequences?"

"You said you wouldn't kill us," Florentine said, her voice rising with panic.

Claude-Michel gave her a look that was almost kind, like a father looking at a very young daughter who is frightened of a monster that doesn't exist. "No," Claude-Michel said. "We won't kill you. But this morning, we are going to give you a demonstration of what will happen if you dare to disobey our wishes." When he spoke the next sentence, his voice became dangerous. "Chloe, come to me."

My stomach boiled with fear. I shook my head. "Claude-Michel—"

"Do what I tell you to do," he said, blinking. "Come to me."

I hugged the carriage door tighter. "But Claude-Michel, you can't mean to—I thought—"

"Chloe!" he shouted. Florentine stopped sobbing. Bernardo swallowed visibly. Even Jean and François jumped. Then Claude-Michel smiled and softened his voice. "If you do not come to me when I ask, it will be much worse. You don't want it to be worse, do you?"

I obeyed, but could not keep my lip from quivering. He took me by the wrists and held me in place. "Jean, if Bernardo or his sister tries to flee, prevent them."

"*Oui, Monsieur,*" Jean said.

"If you fail, you will be whipped."

"*Oui, Monsieur,*" Jean repeated.

"Anyone who tries to flee will be whipped," Claude-Michel said. Florentine moved closer to her brother. "François, retrieve the crop from the carriage and remove her clothing."

François returned from the carriage brandishing the riding crop like a sword. As he walked past them, he glanced down at the brother and sister, who watched him fearfully. There were dark circles under their eyes, but I could tell they were wide awake.

I watched over my shoulder as François approached. Tears coursed down my cheeks, but I did not struggle in Claude-Michel's grip. I felt resigned to my fate.

"Do not move," Claude-Michel cooed as François approached. He let go of my wrists to pull my blouse over my head. Then Claude-Michel took my wrists in his hands again. He looked into my eyes but addressed the brother and sister. "I am your master. You will obey me in all things, or be punished. François is my second, and will have the power to punish as well. Obey him, except where his will conflicts with mine. Chloe has been disrespectful toward François, and now she must suffer the consequences." Claude-Michel shifted his gaze to François. "At your leisure."

I bowed my head. I was not prepared when François brought the crop down ferociously across my shoulders. I could not keep myself from whining like a child as my body shuddered. My hands balled into fists. Claude-Michel held my wrists securely as François brought down the lash again and again. My body struggled. The pain was almost unbearable. Several times, my knees buckled. From somewhere outside of me, I heard François's name.

It was Claude-Michel. "Enough!"

I collapsed against him and sobbed freely in his arms, half from relief that it was over, half because it had happened at all.

"Claude-Michel," François said with a laugh. "You can't mean me to stop now. I've just begun."

"It is enough, François. When you punish them you must remain here in your mind."

"Oh," François said. "Of course."

"If you wish to further demonstrate your mastery over her, you may take her."

I waited, to see what he would say.

"Perhaps later," he said, and walked away.

Chapter Sixteen

A WEEK later we were in Venice.

With the money we had left over, we found a suitable apartment and stabled the horses and carriage. The next day, Claude-Michel used his Venice accounts to purchase new clothes for us all, including servant-wear for Bernardo and Florentine, but not for me, which made François scowl and me laugh. François had insisted on going with him, and suggested that he shouldn't touch his Parisian accounts yet, as he wanted to appear dead.

"Yet, it will be obvious I am not dead when we return to Paris," Claude-Michel said.

"I still have time to convince you not to go," François answered with a wry smile. The rest of us pretended not to hear the conversation—Florentine glancing up from time to time from a book Claude-Michel had bought her, Bernardo pacing the room like an angry tiger, Jean putting away our things. I sat on the couch near Florentine, dividing my attention between watching her read and listening to the men, wondering what in the world was going to happen next.

While they were out, Claude-Michel and François had found the house where that woman Katarina's son lived.

"Paris is a fool's errand," François said in low tones. For once, I agreed with him.

"Perhaps," Claude-Michel replied.

The apartment had two adjoining bedrooms—a master room with a large bed and a room with two smaller ones. François tried to change the subject by suggesting that he and Claude-Michel take the large bed and leave the others to the rest of us.

"No," Claude-Michel said. "Chloe will share my bed. You will be my lieutenant in the servants' room. I want you to take Bernardo into your bed and teach him to please a man. Jean will do the same with Florentine."

I glanced over to see Jean look at him suddenly, unable to disguise the pleasure in his eyes.

François sounded stricken. "Claude-Michel, what are you saying? Did we not agree that we two were the heads of the family? The parents? Shouldn't you and I—?"

Claude-Michel put up an impatient hand. "I don't know what madness has overcome you, François, but I prefer to have a beautiful woman sleeping beside me night after night. Don't make me regret what we have shared recently by acting like a woman instead of a comrade."

François opened his mouth, throwing his hands wide in supplication, then gestured to himself indignantly. "Have you not made use of Jean since he first came to work for you?"

Claude-Michel sounded weary. "Jean is a young man. You, mon ami, are forty-five years old."

"But I am beautiful yet," François said, pouting.

It was true, I had to admit. The turn had erased what gray had been in François' hair, making it much more golden than it had been. He was still a beautiful man. But Claude-Michel was right. There was a masculine hardness to his features that Jean did not yet have.

"Bernardo is beautiful and young," Claude-Michel said. "He will share your bed—" And here he gave a sardonic smile, "—until I call for him. He is mine, after all."

"Yours?" François spat. "What makes you think they can all be yours? What gives you the right to claim everyone?"

"If you wish to challenge me, François..."

François's gaze faltered. By now I knew they had both been soldiers in their youth, and were both very good with weapons and in a fight, but that Claude-Michel had always been the more dominant of the two. From the moment I met them I suspected François would never challenge him, and I was right.

Claude-Michel went to him and placed his hand against his cheek. François took in a breath and nudged against him, closing his eyes without caring who was in the room witnessing the spectacle. Claude-Michel spoke softly. "We are the most powerful of our little family. We have to spread ourselves among our children or they will grow restless. It does not mean I love you less." To my surprise, he kissed François deeply, as I watched with my mouth open.

"Let me go with you tonight," François breathed.

"No, *mon ami*," Claude-Michel said. "Stay here. Lord it over our children. I won't be gone very long."

"But what will you do with this Gypsy boy? Do you think he will suddenly call you papa? He probably wants to kill you."

"He will have a difficult time if that is what he wants," Claude-Michel said. "And now I am going to sleep for a while."

He stretched out on the bed and dozed. I curled up next to him but only pretended to sleep, so I heard François leave, and the brother and sister retire to the other bedroom to whisper and finally fall silent, and still did not move when Jean came to wake Claude-Michel.

"We must hurry, *Monsieur*," Jean said. "The horses are ready."

I felt Claude-Michel sit up and swing his legs over the side of the bed, and opened my eyes in slits. Jean brushed Claude-Michel's hair. The boy had already dressed, in a light blue textured coat to match his coloring, along with a matching blue ribbon. He turned toward me. I closed my eyes quickly.

"We are quite a pair, Jean," Claude-Michel said.

"*Monsieur* Villaforte would not like to hear you say that, *Monsieur*," Jean answered, and I could have sworn I heard a wry smile in his voice. "He is jealous now."

"*Oui*," Claude-Michel said with a flourish of his hand. "François, Chloe. I have too many wives. It is good you are not so jealous."

"Your happiness is my happiness, *Monsieur*," he said.

"Such a loyal servant," Claude-Michel said. "Perhaps Chloe should have turned you instead."

Hearing my name made my heart flutter, even though he was saying it only in passing.

"Where is my old friend?"

"He said he needed to clear his head," Jean said.

Claude-Michel grunted. "Then it falls to Chloe to watch over our beautiful young Italians. She is obviously capable."

I could not resist opening my eyes a little as Jean helped him dress in his new suit—a coat of royal blue with matching ribbon in his hair; new, silver-buckled shoes; white stockings that displayed the impressive curve of his calf. He wore no makeup, saying he did not wish to appear ostentatious, and no wig, preferring to display his natural hair as he claimed the young men now did in Paris. When Claude-Michel was dressed, Jean left to bring around the horses. Claude-Michel inspected himself in the mirror.

"I hope there is some small part of Katarina alive in her son," he said softly. "And I hope there is part of me in him as well."

I could no longer pretend to sleep, especially when private moments with Claude-Michel were so rare. "You are very handsome, *Monsieur*," I said, sitting up.

He turned quickly, with a startled expression on his face. Then he smiled. He came to stand next to the bed, and burrowed his fingers in my hair, tickling my neck. My jaw went slack. I wished I could have him to myself for a while.

"My darling," he said. "You are beautiful in the morning."

"It isn't morning, Claude-Michel." I looked up at him, unable to resist smiling.

"Ah, but the universe revolves around us," he said. "We are the sun that lights its way. As we have just risen, it can be nothing but morning."

For some reason, his teasing only saddened me.

"What is it, *cherie*?"

I shook my head and got out of bed, putting on a covering and throwing open the balcony windows to stand with my hands on the rail. A child ran by a group of men on the street below. From far away, a woman's voice called for Paolo.

"I've grown accustomed to these things quickly," I said. "These windows, and such wonderful fabrics. My husband was never able..." Here I choked. I did not like to let myself think of him, or my children. My memories burned me like fire. "But he loved me."

Claude-Michel came to stand beside me. "You grieve your family as I grieve mine," he said.

I know I looked at him with an expression of surprise. "I tell myself, they are asleep in my mind."

"It is the past," he said quietly. "Our future lies with each other." He placed his fingertips on my chin and gently turned my face to him. "My beautiful Chloe. You gave me this wonderful gift, to see in the darkness. I have only this one errand, this one piece of my past to visit. I have, perhaps, one child left to me. I must know him."

I nodded, though I was perfectly aware there was this, and then his revenge, and then who knew what afterward. But I pretended to believe him in that moment, because he pretended to believe himself. "I understand. But my heart breaks, because—"

"Because why, *cherie*?"

"Because I am falling in love with you." Tears coursed down my cheeks and I let them. "But I would give anything to have found a less complicated man."

He put his arms around me and pulled me to his chest. "Ah, my beautiful Chloe. Yet here we are, together in Venice. And of all the men in the world you could love, only I have the power to promise you forever."

The next moment, Jean was back to steal Claude-Michel away from me once more. And the moment after that, there was an urgent knock at our door.

Chapter Seventeen

GLANCING IN the direction of the small bedroom where the brother and sister slept, I hurried to the door and flung it open before the noise could wake them. It was my first look at Victoire du Fresne.

He was handsome. I thought so from the moment I saw him, with longer hair than Claude-Michel's, pulled back in exactly the same style. His nose was just as impressive, and was one of the things that made me believe him instantly when he said he was Claude-Michel's younger brother, though his build was slight. The thing that convinced me the most, however, was the depth of his dark eyes. It would have been easy to drown there.

"Where is François Villaforte?" he demanded, pushing his way in and looking around. "My brother is rushing into danger he knows nothing about."

At first I fumed at his arrogance. Then I heard his words. "Danger? What are you talking about, danger?"

He turned back to me. "I knew he would come here. This is where he last saw that Gypsy woman from his youth. I have been waiting. And then one night I heard news of him, in a bar. A man talking about how two Parisian nobles and a young boy had escaped him, and so I listened. He has learned about Katarina, and he knows about her son. Claude-Michel's son."

For a moment, time stopped. I went cold inside. "A man—with white hair and skin?"

Victoire—though I didn't know that was his name at the time—froze and looked at me. "Yes. You know this man?"

"We must go," I said. "We have to go warn him."

He looked at me then with the sort of disdain I had seen only on Claude-Michel's face. If I'd had any doubts that they were brothers, they were gone in an instant. "We? This is not something for a woman to do. Where is Villaforte?"

"He is pouting in the streets. This man you speak of…I know him well. I know how dangerous he is. And I am better protection for you than you are for me."

He laughed. "You? Protect me?" His face darkened quickly, and I saw the danger there that so often appeared on Claude-Michel's face. "You are wasting my time," he said darkly, and headed for the door.

Before he reached it, I reached him, and had him pinned against it before he knew what hit him. He struggled, but could not resist. It felt good to have a du Fresne under my power, even if it was to be for just a moment. "There are things you do not know about me, *Monsieur* du Fresne. And things you do not know about your brother. Perhaps *you* rush into danger you don't know enough about."

I let my voice take on the rough edge that only vampires seem to have.

"Obviously," he said. He sounded worried. "Perhaps you can tell me these things in my carriage?"

My heart beat quickly while riding, though not for the obvious reasons. I worried about Claude-Michel, and about Gunnar's presence here, but all the same I felt more than a little relieved that I would get a look at the house he was visiting, and perhaps see this Gypsy boy for myself.

"You know where he is going?"

"I know better than he does. I found it when I first came here."

The Marchesa Antonia Di'Angelo, who had raised Katarina's son, lived in a manor on the outskirts of the city. We stopped the carriage in the woods, a safe distance from the house. When I got out, he tried to keep me from leaving. "We can see them from here," he said. "If anything happens, we will be able to intervene."

"I want to know what is being said. You stay here with your boy. I won't be long." I knew I could move more quickly and quietly than he.

"It is better if we stay together."

"If I were an ordinary woman, *Monsieur*, then I would agree with you. But you will only slow me down and I do not wish to have a burden to defend."

That struck something deep within him. I did not know just how deep at that time. He nodded. "All right. Go. I'll be here if you need me."

I nodded back and moved quickly toward the house. I wondered what I looked like to him as I disappeared through the trees. I also wondered if Gunnar were there somewhere, watching, lying in wait for Claude-Michel as his brother had done.

"Think about what you have to do," I whispered to myself, even though the light sifting through the treetops reminded me of the day I met Gunnar. For that reason if for no other, it seemed the forest was thick with his presence.

I found the window to the front room with ease. Reasoning they would visit there, I retreated into the nearby trees, too far away for a regular human to see and hear, too far for anyone to notice me. Then I waited.

It was quite some time before I heard the crunch of carriage wheels. My heart thumped so loudly in my chest I could barely breathe. Even without Gunnar, I knew there was a good chance of being punished for this. But I could not let myself think about that. Trying to ignore the roar of my own blood in my ears and the frightened nausea that threatened to make me hide among the shadows, I watched their lips and listened.

"Should I come with you, *Monsieur*?" Jean asked hopefully as he opened the carriage door for Claude-Michel.

"No," Claude-Michel said. "I am arriving unannounced. Perhaps it is better if you stay." Jean looked disappointed. Claude-Michel appraised the house. "Perhaps he is not here and we will have to come back," he said. Oddly enough, he sounded as though he hoped it was true.

He squared his shoulders as though he meant to flaunt the half-foot he had gained during the change, and sauntered up the walkway.

A young servant girl answered the door. "I have come to see the Marchesa Antonia Di'Angelo," Claude-Michel said. "If she is in?"

"Of course, *Signore*. Come in," the girl said demurely, and lowered her eyes. Something burned within me at the sight, because I knew he enjoyed her submissive demeanor, and I knew he would take her if he got the chance.

I turned my attention to the window. The curtain was open, so I could see much of the front room. I could also see the marchesa as she reached the bottom of the staircase. She was an elegant woman of perhaps 60 years, who moved with grace and regarded him with curious eyes. There was something about her I liked, but I was glad she was old and not likely to catch Claude-Michel's eye. Halfway down the stairs, she stopped.

"Oh my," she said, and fluttered her hand toward her bosom, then stopped it in mid-air. "I wondered if this day would ever come."

Claude-Michel seemed taken aback by her words. "*Perdone, Madame?*"

"You are the very image of my Lucio."

"Lucio." Claude-Michel whispered the name. Distance and walls muffled their voices. Even with my vampire senses, it was difficult to hear.

The marchesa smiled not unkindly as she studied his face and started down the stairs again. "Forgive me. Katarina spoke often of the handsome young Frenchman she called Claudio. You can be no other than he."

"Yes," he said. "I am Claudio."

There seemed to be some sort of declaration in his voice as he said that name, but at the time I didn't realize the significance—that this moment was the death of le Compte Louis Claude-Michel du Fresne and the birth of a new man. A man without title or responsibility to any but his new family.

The marchesa cocked her head to one side. I could tell something young still burned inside of her. "Please come in and sit," she said, and led the way to the parlor. "There has been no one these many years with whom I could reminisce about my wild, spirited friend Katarina. I lost a great deal of social standing for some time just by associating with her. But I didn't care. Through her stories, I lived such a life—music and dancing, and making love beneath the stars."

She motioned to a spot on the couch, waving a hand as she lowered herself onto the other end. "Oh, I know you came to meet your son, not reminisce with some old woman. Lucio will be home within the hour. And there is no doubt that he is your son."

Claude-Michel smiled. "Time spent in the company of a beautiful woman is always a pleasure," he said with a look of mischief and slight bow of the head. His nervousness vanished.

The marchesa gave a hearty laugh. "Oh you are a charmer, aren't you? Twenty years ago that would have been the truth, and maybe I would have given Katarina a contest for your affections. Esperanza," she said to the servant-girl. "Something to drink for our guest. And myself."

He lowered his eyelids enticingly. "She spoke of me?"

"Often. She loved you."

Claude-Michel didn't answer right away. I could tell he struggled with emotions, and I was not prepared for the way I felt, seeing him still so enthralled by the memory of a woman with whom I doubted I would ever be able to compete. I saw longing, tenderness and regret on his face, things I never saw when he looked at me. But I was here to protect him from Gunnar, I reminded myself, and swallowed my feelings.

"How did you become friends?" he finally asked.

The old woman smiled. "We met at the market when some of her troupe came to town. Her belly had just started to grow round with Lucio. I was thirty-nine, near the same age as she, and I was intrigued. She was quick to lash out at the men who taunted her, and just as quick to laugh. She was nothing like the stilted women I called my friends. Those proper women. I'm sure you know the type."

Claude-Michel nodded, and smiled politely. I knew he wanted her to say more about Katarina.

"I tolerated them for the sake of having someone to talk to," the marchesa said. "But Katarina—from the beginning it seemed we were sisters." She paused long enough to accept her glass of wine from her servant Esperanza, and took a sip. The way she seemed to be thinking through her memories reminded me of someone rifling through old letters.

"Of course, I enjoyed the scandalized reactions of my equals as much as I enjoyed Katarina's company. I would sneak out of the city and meet her in the fields. My husband was in ill health and did not have the strength to enforce his wishes that I not see this Gypsy. She taught me to ride a horse like a man, and to smoke. And once, I even kissed her brother. I think that is what frightened me. I didn't go back. Instead, I went home, pretended to be a good wife, and stayed with my husband until he died. By that time Katarina and her people had moved on. I didn't see her for three years. Then one day, she came and found me."

"A man told me there was a sickness," Claudio said.

The marchesa nodded. "There was. Katarina was not yet ill, but many of her family were. She wanted me to take care of Lucio until it had passed. At least that is what she told me. I don't think she really expected to survive. She didn't, after all. Not many of them did."

"I'm sorry," Claude-Michel said. "I had hoped to find her."

The old woman nodded sympathetically. "I still think about her often. And I see her spirit in Lucio—that temper that can rage one moment only to be replaced by laughter the next." She chuckled a little to herself. "One does not easily forget someone like Katarina. But then, I'm sure you know that."

"Yes," Claude-Michel said. "She has been with me these many years."

The marchesa's inquisitive gaze became shrewd. "I would ask you—what suddenly brings you to look for her?"

Suddenly, I heard hoof beats from someplace behind me. I nearly panicked. Then I remembered this Lucio was expected home any minute. Claude-Michel momentarily lost his focus on the old woman, glancing briefly over his shoulder, then smiled at her again. She showed no signs of having heard the hoof beats, though they were coming closer.

"A man sees things changing around him and realizes he is growing older," Claude-Michel said.

"You married."

"Yes."

The marchesa turned her head toward the door. "Ah, there's Lucio now," she said, as his horse approached the stable at a gallop. An aging stable hand came out to take him. The horse leapt a few inches off the ground with its front hooves as Lucio dismounted.

He was beautiful, like Claude-Michel and his brother. Though he was perhaps twenty-five years old and slightly built, he carried himself powerfully, as a much older, much larger man would. He had Claude-Michel's prominent nose and bottomless black eyes. His skin was much darker, however, an olive tone, his lips full and sensual. His head was ringed by a mass of long, black curls reaching just below his shoulders.

He did not stand on ceremony, but burst into the house.

I shifted my gaze back to the window to see Claude-Michel stand.

"Lucio," the old woman said gently. "This is—"

"Claudio du Fresne," Claude-Michel finished. "I'm—"

"My father?" Lucio said, removing his hat. "Yes, I can see that is probably true. Did you know you are the one person besides Mama who can ruin my reputation by telling the world I'm half Gypsy?" He sauntered over to Claude-Michel and looked him over. "I would kill you on the spot if I gave a damn about anything," he said, and turned on his heel toward the servant-girl, who had suddenly blanched. "Esperanza," he said, "where is my Chartreuse, eh?"

"I'm sorry, *Signore*," the girl said, and fled the room.

"I told you what would happen the next time you forgot!" he called after her, then spun back on his toe with a devilish grin. "Poor thing, she's frightened to death of me, but I haven't the slightest idea why." To Claude-Michel, he said, "I did very well for myself, don't you think? It is very lucky for you I didn't grow up in squalor." He moved with a dangerous, playful energy.

Even from so far away, I could see Claude-Michel blinking rapidly, as he did when he was caught off-guard. "I didn't know about you," he said. "When I discovered you had been born, I came immediately."

"News travels very slowly," Lucio said as Esperanza hurried back with a tray containing a bottle of light green liquid and a small glass, which she filled and handed to Lucio. "Ah," he said. "Very nice." He raised the glass to Claude-Michel. "Chartreuse. It's the French in me, I suppose," he said, and drank. "What is my legacy then? No one ever told me your position in the world. I imagine you failed to mention that to my mother, as a precaution so that she would not be able to find you. I imagine you married well."

"Yes," Claude-Michel said quietly, and glanced briefly at the marchesa, but she was looking at her son.

"Good," Lucio said. "Let's all drink to my stepmother, Mrs. du Fresne—"

Anger flashed across Claude-Michel's face. "She's dead," he said in a low warning tone. "I loved her very much. You also had a brother named Gabriel, and a sister, Camille. Also dead. Both of them."

Lucio stopped in his tracks and the two men regarded each other—father looking darkly upon son, son regarding father with a look of sobering realization. "I have a daughter," he offered. "I married well also. Perhaps in time I will love my wife."

"A daughter..." Claude-Michel said. "I have a granddaughter?"

"Francesca Katarina. My wife thinks Katarina is a long-lost favorite aunt of Mama's. They are staying with her relatives in the country."

"She's a beautiful child," the marchesa said. "I know you will think so."

Lucio approached Claude-Michel with a grin. "You owe me wine," he said. "A glass for each year you waited to find me, eh?" He drank the rest of the Chartreuse and set the glass on the table, meeting Esperanza's gaze as he did so. "Expect a visit from me later," he said to her. Then he headed for the door with a flourish of his hand. "Come with me to my favorite tavern. We will decide if we want to be father and son."

"But of course," Claude-Michel said. "My man is waiting outside. We will take my carriage."

I hurried back through the forest as quickly and quietly as I could.

Chapter Eighteen

"QUICKLY!" I shouted from the forest, then looked Victoire in the eye before I could get the rest out. He recoiled against the carriage and looked around, as if some answer were in the trees. The boy who drove him looked on with wide, curious eyes. "They are going to Lucio Di'Angelo's favorite tavern."

"*La Piuma Nera,*" he said.

"We have to go," I said. He nodded and came to his senses, climbing into the carriage and ordering his boy to the tavern.

Once we were traveling, however, he looked at me strangely. "What are you?" he asked, a lot more matter-of-factly than I would have expected.

"Things have happened," I said. "There are things you don't know about your brother, and about this man who is looking for him. That man's name is Gunnar, and he is a pirate. I was his captive for many months. He was going to kill Claude-Michel. I couldn't let him do that."

"So you just...escaped?"

"I am stronger than I look," I said.

"I think you will owe me an explanation when we are with him."

"I think you should ask your brother. I don't owe you anything. I have never seen you before."

At the door to *La Piuma Nera,* I held Victoire back. Of course, he was not happy about being ordered around by a woman, but he was still curious and wary enough to listen for the moment. "Shh!" I whispered. "I want to listen."

"Does your young wife know yet of your trysts?" Claudio asked the boy as I slipped inside and hid myself in nearby shadows. Claudio looked around but did not see me. The young man soon recaptured his attention. My attention was so captured by the two of them, I was not able to place the sharp animal tang of sweat that I mistook for the general smell of the bar.

Lucio shrugged. Then he smiled wickedly. "Once, she was furious with me for returning home with my clothes reeking of the whorehouse. She threw a sachet at me." He slapped a hand against his chest and spoke in mock indignation.

"Wives do shocking things," Claude-Michel said with a sly grin I was learning to love and hate at the same time.

"She was the one shocked. I don't think she had ever been spanked before that day, but her bottom was a nice rosy color when I'd finished. I made such love to her afterward. I find it an effective way to keep her from making demands. A pink bottom will make a woman forget her jealousies quickly."

Claude-Michel laughed. It was the first real laugh I had heard him utter. "There is no doubt about it," he said, and clapped the boy on the back. "You are my son."

"Of course," Lucio said. "And I am very glad to know who bears the blame for this," he said, running a finger down the length of his nose. Then he banged on the bar. "Oy!" He called. "Niko!"

A smiling older man appeared from a back room.

"The devil has returned!" the man said in a Greek accent, coming around the bar to give Lucio a crushing hug. His gaze fell then on Claudio, and his eyes grew large as he looked from one to the other. "An older brother?"

"A father," Lucio said. Lucio square his shoulders with pride as he spoke.

"Raised from the dead!"

Lucio tapped his lips with a finger. "It depends on which story I've told you."

"I've known you too long," Niko said, waddling back around the bar and waving Lucio away. "I've heard all of your stories, even the ones that are true." He leaned on the bar toward Claudio. "When he was a little boy, he caused me all kinds of trouble. Such a little demon." He shrugged. "But he is good for business. Everyone comes to see what the devil-boy is up to today—friends, enemies. And now," he said, pulling down a bottle of amber-colored liquor and three glasses. "Something on the house. Today, we celebrate a reunion between father and son."

From deeper within the tavern, someone spoke in a voice that was aging, yet resonant, in an accent dead for many, many generations. "Today...we celebrate many reunions."

Then Gunnar was in front of Claudio, holding firmly to the blade of his rapier. Behind me, Victoire lumbered in awkwardly, also with a rapier in hand. I put myself between Claudio's brother and the man I had hoped never to see again.

Gunnar's white eyes stared deeply into Claudio's black ones as thick rivulets of blood ran down his arm. "You can't kill me," Gunnar said, narrowing his eyes. "But, yes...I can see you would like to very much."

He pawed the blade to the side. Claude-Michel went for his heart and found himself rushing only air as Gunnar stood to the side, laughing.

"What demon is this?" Niko asked, crossing himself. Lucio stood with his hand on the hilt of his sword, looking around wildly, his wide eyes settling on Claudio's face. Claudio stood breathing through his open mouth, paying no attention to the fangs growing past the concealment of his upper lip.

"What *are* you?" Lucio demanded, as Victoire had demanded of me not half an hour before.

Gunnar laughed loudly, showing his fangs, bellowing, "He is what I am. A defiler of all that is pure. But... you haven't told your long-lost son of your adventures on board my ship, and how a young French beauty turned you into what you are today."

I heard Victoire gasp behind me and wondered if he was about to run me through with his weapon.

Gunnar clicked his tongue. "It isn't good to have such secrets between father and son. Especially when you've been away for so long." Then he spoke to me without turning around. "I know you're there, Chloe. I know everything that happens around me."

I couldn't keep myself from responding. "I should have cut off your head and fed it to the sharks, as I dreamed of doing every night."

"What have you done?" Victoire whispered behind me, but to this day I don't know who he was talking to. Himself, perhaps.

In spite of what was happening around him, Claudio looked calm, yet coiled. I knew even then he was a man accustomed to conflict. The boy, on the other hand, seemed wild in comparison, though he had managed to slip a dagger from his boot. We all waited to see what would happen next, watching this terrible white-maned man who seemed so much more than human—so much more, even, than vampire.

"Oh, yes," Gunnar said, turning so that his back was no longer to me and Victoire. "I know about you as well, Claude-Michel. I know all about you. More than you can imagine. And I know about your friend François, and your children."

"You don't know about me," Lucio spat. Gunnar turned toward him with an arrogant grin, meeting the flying dagger blade with his eye. He froze, and the confident look fled his face. His remaining eye went wild as thick, dark bands of blood ran down his cheek. I could do nothing except watch in shocked horror. With a scream of rage, he groped blindly at his face, then went down on his knees. He tried to rise, and then slid to a sitting position, gasped, and fell backward. As he lay twitching, he turned his face toward Claudio.

"You can't...kill...me..." he rasped. With a cry of rage, Claudio drove his rapier into Gunnar's remaining eye, careful to avoid the spurt of blood. Gunnar screamed and grabbed the blade, tearing his fingers to ribbons, spraying droplets. Finally, he stopped moving, and Claudio bent over him.

"Don't ever underestimate me," Claudio hissed between his teeth. Then he braced against Gunnar's chest with his boot to reclaim his weapon and Lucio's, wiping the blades on the fallen man's breeches as Gunnar moved his hands aimlessly. Lucio gingerly accepted his dagger, but gave Claudio a suspicious look.

Claudio had already headed for the door by the time Niko started screaming, "Get out! Get out of here!"

"Come on!" Claudio shouted, without stopping to see if anyone obeyed. Outside, Lucio challenged him. "That man," he said. "That man...what was he?"

"Yes, Diable, who was he?" Victoire echoed.

Claudio looked at both of us darkly. "Vampire," he said.

"Vampire?" Lucio whispered. "But... it isn't possible."

"It is," Claudio said.

"And you?" Lucio said, leaning in close.

"No," Claude-Michel said, smiling carefully. "Men say things when they are upset. Monsters do even more."

It gave me such a strange feeling to hear him say that, but I blamed it on the circumstance, assumed he planned to explain everything to his son when emotions were no longer so violent.

Without warning, Lucio lashed out. Claudio caught his wrists before the boy's hands could come in contact with his face, and had him pinned against his carriage. Jean watched from his driver's perch, clearly wanting to come down and defend his master.

"Show me," Lucio demanded. "Show me your teeth."

Claudio relaxed. His fangs had just started to recede from his encounter with Gunnar. Now they were long again, ready if need be to sink into Lucio's flesh.

"Show me!" Lucio shouted.

"No," Claude-Michel said. The sharp tips revealed themselves even as he spoke.

Lucio tried to struggle away. "It's true!" he said, terror and rage at war on his face. Claudio let him go and stood scowling at the boy.

"Is this why you came to see me?" Lucio demanded, eyes and hair wild. "You want to make me what you are? What that hideous man back there is?"

"No," Claudio said. "I would not take from you your life—your wife and daughter. I would not do that!" He brought his hand hard against the side of the carriage, by the boy's head, and turned his back, breathing heavily.

Lucio jumped, but recovered quickly and followed him. "How do I know this? I have never seen you before today. How do I know what you would do?"

Claudio turned and shouted, "Do not judge me by what has happened to me! Judge me by my actions. From what you've told me, they are not so different from your own. We are the same."

Lucio moved away, eyes wide. "Blood," he said, holding up his hand. "You drink blood?"

Suddenly, Claudio looked like the most weary man in the world. "Yes," he said with a sigh.

Wild-eyed, Lucio nodded, then bent over and gagged. Claudio took a step toward him, but Lucio moved away. "Don't come near me!" he shouted, standing up with some difficulty. "Don't ever come near me! Stay away from me and from my family," he said. "Whatever else I've done, I am not yet damned to hell."

Claudio spoke quietly. "Allow me, at least, to return you to your home—"

"I'll find my own way home," Lucio said, backing away. Then he turned and ran toward the road.

Claudio watched him go for a moment. Then he turned to Victoire. "If you are not repulsed by vampires, brother, ride with us in my carriage. Instruct Pierre to follow."

Victoire's eyes were still very wide, but he nodded and went to speak with his boy. Claudio turned to Jean. "Take us home," he said, his voice breaking. "There is nothing more for me here tonight."

* * * *

"You're both vampires," Victoire said hesitantly in the carriage. He sat across from me and Claudio, in the middle of the bench, facing backward.

"Yes," Claudio said wearily. "It was necessary, thanks to our albino friend. You are in no danger. We feed on human slaves."

Victoire nodded. No one said anything else until we arrived at the apartment.

Florentine was sitting on the couch in the drawing room, brushing her hair, while François stared down into the street from the balcony. He came in when he heard us. Florentine sat still and looked nervously at everyone.

"Where is Bernardo?" Claudio demanded.

"Sulking," François said, then flashed his most winning smile at Claudio and Victoire. "Victoire, it has been too long. And how is the pride of your loins?" he asked Claudio, then squinted at him. "What is that on your cuffs?"

Claudio looked at the brown stain on his cuffs. "My son is alive and well," Claudio said. "His name is Lucio. Why is Bernardo sulking?"

"I was hungry and there was a fire between my legs."

"It's probably syphilis," Claudio said, rubbing his eyes with thumb and forefinger.

"We can't get syphilis," François said, turning to me. "Can we?"

"I haven't been ill since changing, and I never saw Gunnar become ill, either," I said.

"What an interesting life my brother has been leading," Victoire said, stepping further into the room.

"Never say that devil's name," he said, raising his finger at me.

"Claude-Michel...is something wrong?" François asked.

"Forget that name as well," he said. "Claude-Michel is dead, and we have to leave this place." To Jean, he said, "Pack our things. You help him," he said to Pierre.

Pierre looked at his master, who nodded.

François looked strangely at Claudio. "To whom am I speaking, then?"

"Claudio du Fresne. From now on, call me that. Claude-Michel is dead," he repeated, absently touching the place over his heart with a stray hand. "Florentine, go get your brother and tell him it is time to go." She screwed up her face and threw down her book, then fled to the small bedroom.

François glanced at her briefly, then turned his attention back to Claudio. He looked worried. "Claude-Michel...what is it?" he asked.

Claudio smiled and batted his eyes at the other man. "I said not to call me that."

François furrowed his brow. "What is wrong, *mon ami*?" he asked. "Why do we have to leave?"

"Gunnar is here."

François' jaw dropped. "Gunnar?" he repeated, closing his right hand as though clutching an imaginary sword. "How?"

"I accompanied my son to a tavern, and he was there. I didn't even hear him walk behind me."

François narrowed his eyes. "Where is he now, Claude-Mich—*merde*! Where is he now?"

"We killed him, my son Lucio and I. In the tavern."

"He's right," Victoire said. "I came to warn him, but he had already gone."

By then, Florentine and a cross-looking Bernardo were standing in the doorway.

I shook my head. "I don't believe he is dead. He's too—"

"We killed him!" Claudio shouted, advancing on me, gesturing. "His brain is full of holes."

"There will be an inquiry," François said.

Claudio nodded. "Yes."

"Where is your son now?" François asked.

"Gone," Claudio said. "Gone from my life forever."

François' expression was a mixture of pity and relief. The next moment, he sprang into action, clapping his hands. "Move quickly, pets. We have to go. Especially you, Jean. I need you to get everything down to the carriage and be prepared to drive through the night."

Jean looked at his master, who sat on the couch with a hand over his eyes. Claudio waved his hand vaguely in the air. "Do what he says," he told him. Jean nodded and did as he was told.

For some reason, I was frozen to the spot as though I wasn't even there. François noticed this. "Come on, come on!" he told me. "Get your things."

I glanced back as Victoire sat beside Claudio to ask what he could do, then pulled myself together and obeyed, part of me hating that I did what François said so readily. He followed me into the small bedroom, where Florentine was face down on the bed, sobbing.

I went to her. "What's wrong?" I asked. Bernardo stood by looking horrified.

"What's going on?" François demanded. "Did you not hear what I told you to do?"

Florentine flipped over and scowled at him. "I don't want to get my things!" she shouted. "We just got here after two weeks in that horrible carriage. I want to stay here for a while."

"We can't stay here right now," I said, glancing at François. "We do have to go quickly."

François was across the room in a moment. He pulled Florentine off the bed and forced her to look at him. "There are things at work here that you don't understand," he said. "It is vitally important that you do what you're told."

Florentine glared at him. "Why?" she spat. "Are you afraid the villagers will come with wooden stakes?"

I recognized the anger in François' face and hurried around the bed to grab his arm. "No, François," I said. "She's just frightened."

He froze and narrowed his eyes. "Take your hand off, or so help me, you will be next."

For a moment, I didn't move, unable to admit to myself that he frightened me almost as much as Claudio did. But in the end, the threat of punishment did its trick, and I let him have her. Florentine's eyes grew wide and she tried to move away, but he flipped her over the side of the bed with her bottom in the air before she could squeal. He pulled up her skirts unceremoniously and bared her bottom as Bernardo looked on in horror. François raised his hand high and spanked her hard, ignoring her crying and pleas for him to stop. When he finished, he turned to Bernardo, who lowered his eyes and began to hurriedly grab his things.

Sobbing, Florentine straightened her skirts.

"Because you were told to," François said, and stalked from the room.

"What happened in there?" I heard Claudio ask.

"Florentine doesn't think it necessary to take orders from vampires," he said. "But she understands the urgency now." There was a pause, and then: "I will take care of everything for you, *mon ami*."

* * * *

Jean asked where he was to drive.

"We will have to book passage on a ship," Claudio said. "We are going to Paris."

Jean pressed his lips together, nodded, and shot François and Victoire a look.

François blinked rapidly and tried to smile. "But Claude-Michel, we—"

"This has been the plan, François," Claudio said impatiently. "When we finished with Katarina's son, we would return to Paris." He then looked at his brother.

"I am with you, whatever you decide," Victoire said.

"It is good someone is," he said, and climbed into the carriage.

François did not try to hide his anger, pacing and gesturing as he spoke. "I just don't think, after all you've been through, Paris is the place to go. What if someone recognizes you? What if the peasants want your head? What if they want *my* head?"

"Are you suddenly going to become a coward?" Claudio asked. "Were you not onboard Gunnar's ship with me to see what he is capable of? Tonight, with a dagger in his eye, he spoke to me."

François growled in frustration and climbed in after him. "I do not like this, Claude-Michel."

"We will go at night. We have advantages after the sun goes down."

"If you insist," François said.

The rest of us were already inside, Bernardo gazing silently out the back window as Florentine huddled against me, beside him. Victoire had abandoned his carriage, and now he and his boy sat across from Claudio and François. I watched them. I should have known by the strange smile that came to François' face later that day that he was up to something.

* * * *

That evening, when we stopped at an inn to rest the horses, François cheerfully opened a bottle of wine in the room after Bernardo, Florentine and Pierre went to bed. Jean remained with us, sitting at Claudio's feet while his master absently stroked his hair. Victoire watched Pierre go with some regret, I thought, and I wondered just how much the two brothers had in common, whether Victoire used his driver in the same way Claudio used Jean, and whether he was quick to punish. Then I wondered what Victoire tasted like and had to turn my attention elsewhere.

"What is it like?" Victoire wanted to know. "Being a vampire?"

Claudio leaned forward, squeezing a fist. "I am strong, Victoire. Stronger than I have ever been. And larger. You see for yourself."

Victoire nodded. "You cannot eat...food?"

"I don't know," Claudio said. "I have not tried. Wine, I have tried, and I still love the taste of it."

Victoire handed him a bit of bread and Claudio accepted, biting into it and chewing thoughtfully. "It is good still. But when I am hungry, I can think of nothing but the taste of a beautiful neck."

"Interesting," Victoire said, and accepted a glass of wine from François.

"Still," François said. "I have heard that wine does strange things to vampires."

Everyone turned to him. "Like what?" I asked.

"Well...such as...going to their heads quickly. It is an occasional thing and nothing to be alarmed about."

"Where have you heard this?" Claudio asked, taking his glass from François.

"I once heard this long ago. But of course, I paid it no mind, because I did not think vampires existed." François took his own glass and sat with us, watching Claudio closely.

Claudio did not drink. Instead, a strange expression came over his face as he sniffed his wine. He turned a dark look on François and lowered the glass to the tea table, and was in front of the other man in less than a second. Claudio took François' glass out of his hands and sipped from it, giving him a sardonic smile. "It is very good, yes? Mine is not so good."

François tried to move out of his chair, but he did not move fast enough to escape the back of Claudio's hand across his cheek, which caused him to lose his balance and fall to the floor, rubbing the blood from his lip. Jean was on his feet, watching attentively, ready to spring into action.

Without thinking, I moved away, toward Victoire. "Claude-Michel!" I cried. "What are you doing?" Already I could feel my fangs growing.

Victoire was quickly on his feet with a rapier in his hand.

"What are you trying to do?" Claudio bellowed. "Are you thinking to make me sleep so you will have control of our little family?"

François shook his head. "Claude-Michel, I am only concerned for you. I want you to rest well after your ordeal. I don't want you to be forced to think and plan."

"Then you suggest to me that I sleep, not ply me with potions!"

Victoire stood behind François, rapier pointed at the other man's neck, glancing at Claudio for instruction.

François turned his head just a fraction, but kept his attention on Claudio. "I am sorry, Claude-Michel, I—"

"Get up," Claudio said.

"What are you going to do?"

"Do what my brother says," Victoire ordered.

François stood carefully, trying to turn toward Victoire, who pressed the tip of his blade against his back. So he kept an eye on Claudio instead. Claudio picked up his own wine and handed François the poisoned glass. "Tell me, my *friend*," Claudio said significantly. "What are these changes that have come over you? You have not been yourself these past months."

"I've told you everything, Claude-Michel," he said. "Now that our lives are different, I want to show my love for you."

"Why do you suddenly want this, hm?"

François sighed heavily. It seemed as though something in him wilted. "I have always wanted it. I did not take action in the past, because of Angelique. And your children. Now, I see no reason to restrain myself."

Claudio's eyes glittered menacingly. I watched from the corner of the couch, with my feet under my body, ready to spring away at any moment. "When I was in *La Piuma Nera*," Claudio said, "that albino fiend said something very interesting. He said he knew all about you, François. Of course, I didn't have the opportunity to speak with him further about it."

"I don't have any idea what he meant," François said. "That man is evil. He would have said anything."

"Drink your wine," Claudio said darkly. "Or I will pour it down your throat."

François drank it quickly, keeping angry eyes on Claudio. Finished, he set the glass down hard, cracking the base. "There," he said. "Anything to make you happy."

Claudio drained his own glass and went to François, undressing him roughly. Victoire's eyes grew wide, as I'm sure my own did, but he held his sword steady. François' eyes widened as well, but the next moment he tried to touch Claudio, who slapped him hard across the cheek a second time. François gave him a bewildered look.

Without warning, Claudio went into the bedroom and returned with his riding crop. François laughed. "A vampire can take so much more than a mere mortal," he said.

"A vampire can give so much more than a mere mortal…*mon ami*," he said and struck him savagely across the shoulders. François fell to his knees and seemed powerless to rise again as Claudio whipped him until lines of blood criss-crossed his back.

I heard Bernardo and Florentine whispering in the other room, curious about what was happening, while Pierre implored them in French not to come in here. It was wise advice.

"It appears your plan would have failed anyway," Claudio said. "As your sleeping potion has had no effect on you. The next time you do something like this, I will flay you alive."

François looked up at him. Claudio threw the crop to the floor beside him and headed for the door.

"Where are you going, Claude…Claudio?" I asked.

"To have my dinner," he said. "I will return shortly. Don't let him bleed on anything." With that he went out and slammed the door.

I looked at Jean and discovered he was looking at me as well. "Why don't you go with him?" I said. "He is not thinking clearly."

Jean nodded, sheathed his sword, and followed Claudio. I hoped he was moving slowly enough for Jean to catch up. Then I looked down at François, who was just lying there, looking at nothing in particular, his eyes shining with tears.

"Help me get him to the couch," I said.

François shook us off. "I can walk," he said crossly. He lumbered to the couch and collapsed face down, still looking at nothing.

"I'll get a cloth," Victoire said, and disappeared into the bedroom. While he was gone, I inspected François' wounds.

"What are you trying to do?" I asked, feeling genuinely terrible for him.

"I am trying to make him love me," he said.

"And you know him so much better than I do. Even I could have told you this wasn't the way."

When Victoire returned I bathed the blood from François' wounds. Except for twitching his back from time to time, he didn't react at all, though I know it must have hurt very much.

"You are very good at that," Victoire said, cocking his head and smiling at me. I tried not to notice what a beautiful smile he had. It was strange to be surrounded by so much male beauty.

"Thank you," I said.

He took the cloth away and put it on the table, then picked up our two full glasses, and began walking toward the bedroom. "Come with me," he said. "We should give him space to rest."

I obeyed, feeling ridiculous for shivering in the presence of a man who was not a vampire. But he was a du Fresne, and that made all the difference.

He led me into the bedroom and shut the door. "There is something I am curious about," he said, going across the room and sitting in the reading chair. He crossed his legs and regarded me with a much different expression than I had seen from him. It was fraught with a stern challenge.

"What is it?" I asked, staying where I was, sipping from my glass.

"It is obvious you still enjoy wine," he said. "Do you still enjoy other things as well?"

He seemed so much like Claudio in that moment that I nearly gasped.

"Yes," I said.

"Tell me something else," he continued, sipping from his own glass. "Has he punished you yet?"

The question startled me. My mouth went dry. "Yes," I whispered.

"Do you like it? Being with a man who does these things, I mean."

I had to drop my gaze then. I did not know how to answer a question like that.

"It's a simple enough question," he said, standing and putting his wine on the dressing table without taking his eyes off me. He moved toward me slowly, like a cat stalking prey. "Do you like being with a man who takes what he wants...and punishes disobedience?"

I could no longer make myself look at him. I wanted to flee the room. My fangs had again begun to grow. "*Monsieur*," I said, as he took my glass from me and set it next to his. "I am with your brother—"

"Do you think my brother hasn't enjoyed my wife on many occasions?"

I swallowed. I did not know how to respond. "I...did not know you had a wife."

"I do," he said. "But she is not half as beautiful as you."

"That's a terrible thing to say," I told him.

"It is true. Our marriage is an arrangement. And I know my brother will not mind sharing his vampire beauty with me. He has already shared you with others, yes? François?"

"François is not interested in women," I said.

Something twitched in Victoire's face. Then he forced himself to smile. "Of course. But I am."

And with that he took my face in his hands and kissed me roughly, cutting his tongue on one of my teeth. He did not seem to notice, but invaded my mouth, pushing me toward the bed. I pulled away. It seemed far more difficult than it should have.

"Victoire, you should not tease vampires."

"I am not teasing," he said, removing his blouse to show off a thin but muscular physique, and hair more sparse than his brother's. There was something dangerous in his eyes.

"I could kill you easily," I warned.

"But you won't," he said, and pushed me onto the bed, lifting my skirts and penetrating me quickly. I looked into his face, astonished. He looked at me with such arrogant intensity, I wanted to slap him. The little smile on his lips especially made me want this. But any power I had with him, such as the power to make him stay with his carriage at the *marchesa*'s manor, was gone. It had perhaps never been there in the first place. He was Claudio's brother, after all.

He took me hard. I wondered if it was to impress me with his mortal strength, or whether he was simply demonstrating his dominance, but it didn't matter. His thrusting, and the smoky look in his eye, excited me. For a moment, I desperately wanted him to be a vampire so he would be able to take what he wanted from me without question, to make me fear him.

He was, apparently, thinking similar thoughts.

Victoire maneuvered me to the middle of the bed and lay on top of me, breathing into my ear, teasing me with the smell of his flesh and the throb of his veins. I could hear the rush of blood inside of him. My fangs were fully extended. I wanted a taste.

"Make me as you are," he whispered. "I want to be a vampire."

I stopped moving and pushed him up off of me. He looked at my hand, flaring his nostrils, then looked into my eyes. "What are you saying?" I asked.

"You heard me."

"I can not. And I won't."

"You will," he said, squeezing my shoulders painfully.

It didn't take much strength to throw him off me. He landed on his *derriere* and looked around, surprised. Then, his face dark with anger, he stood. By then I was on my feet and facing him. "I am not in phase, Victoire. A vampire cannot make another vampire unless she is in phase. Which I am not."

He nodded and pressed his lips together, then looked at me with a sheepish smile. "I'm sorry, I...got a little over excited. You will forgive me?"

I looked at him warily, but nodded. "I forgive you. But I think I'd better go to bed now. I'm sure Claude-Michel will not be in the best of moods when he returns."

Chapter Nineteen

VICTOIRE CONTINUED to travel with us and François continued to sulk. We arrived at Claudio's manor several weeks later, long after midnight. It seemed too still. I shivered as Claudio gazed up. When I looked at him, I had the strangest sensation I was looking at a ghost. Jean stopped the carriage in front of the door, and Claudio got out, instructing everyone to come with him.

François did not move. "I will help Jean with the horses," he said. Bernardo and Florentine looked at each other.

"No," Claudio said. "You wanted to be by my side. That is where I want you now."

François looked around uneasily, then nodded once and tried to smile.

I stepped out of his way as he climbed from the carriage. "This place is yours?" I asked Claudio.

"Yes," he said. "Draw your weapon," he told François as he drew his own.

François looked at him strangely. "What?"

"We don't know who may be in there," Claudio said impatiently.

"Oh. Yes," François said, and drew his rapier. Claudio opened the door and led the way into the house.

"Bernardo, light that," he said, meaning the candle stub in the brass holder by the door. Within moments, shadows loomed in the corridor. François looked around wildly.

"You were the last one here," Claudio said. "You will help me discover who did this."

François nodded. "Yes, Claude-Michel," he said.

Claudio prowled the house, looking as though he were ready to run through anyone he discovered there, but we found only one empty room after another. Claudio paused in the parlor, waiting for Jean's return, keying the piano. "We had so many conversations in this room," he said.

"Yes," François agreed. "Many."

I thought it was strange that François was being so very quiet.

Florentine and Bernardo kept close to me. "It is a beautiful house, Claudio," I said.

"*Merci*," he muttered. The front door opened. He strode into the corridor, brandishing his weapon.

"It is me, *Monsieur*," Jean said.

"Come on," Claudio said, and headed for the stairs. "We'll make sure no one is upstairs. The house has been empty for a long time."

He made me remain downstairs with the feeders while he took François, Victoire and Jean upstairs. It wasn't long before he called me. There was so much emotion in his voice I thought I must be hearing things.

I was not prepared for what he had found.

Claudio was in one of the upstairs bedrooms, staring at a dusty bed. At first I didn't know what I was looking at, then the frail form of a girl took shape. I thought it must be a ghost or a vision. Then it moved. When the vision opened its eyes, it didn't appear to see, though the candlelight made them sparkle like jewels. A look of confusion passed over the face. My heart beat rapidly as her eyes settled on Claudio, and then grew wide.

"Papa?"

Tears filled my eyes for them as Claudio went to her, touching her forehead with a tenderness I had never before seen from human or vampire.

"Are you a ghost?" she asked.

"A ghost—" he repeated. "Oh, my beautiful flower."

"They said you were dead, Papa."

"Who did, little one?"

"Monsieur Villaforte. He said you'd been killed and that your body was cut to pieces by angry peasants. We buried you next to Gabriel."

Claudio clenched his jaw. His voice came out strained. "Monsieur Villaforte told you this?"

She nodded. "He said he had to leave, but that he would be back."

"Where is your mama?" he asked.

The girl's lip trembled. "She died weeks ago. The sickness—"

"Weeks...she died weeks ago?"

She nodded, coughing. "If you're not dead, where have you been?" she asked when she'd caught her breath.

He bent over and gathered her in his arms. She looked like a skeleton. "Oh, *papillon*, I never would have left you. I thought you were dead. I thought Angelique was dead. Do you have food?"

She shook her head. "Maurice hasn't come yet. He has to go away and find money, but I think...I think he's sick, too."

"Maurice. He left Maurice to care for you?"

She nodded. "Maurice and his wife. But his wife died before Mama. A doctor came, but when Maurice went to get him for Mama, he found that he had died and the other doctors wouldn't come."

"The doctors wouldn't come," he repeated. "We'll see about that. After I speak with Monsieur Villaforte, we're going to find something for you to eat, yes? My friend Chloe will remain with you until I return."

She looked at me. I tried to smile at her. "You're very beautiful," Camille said, and my heart broke instantly in two.

"Not half as beautiful as you," I said.

Claudio stood. I couldn't help but follow. François was in the hallway, looking ill. He took a step back at Claudio's approach. "Don't listen to her, Claude-Michel. She's feverish."

Claudio grabbed him by the front of his coat and sneered into his face. "Don't listen to my daughter? I should not have listened to you! You told me she was dead. I don't think she's so feverish she only thinks that she isn't."

Though he still held his rapier, François opened his arms in supplication. "Claude-Michel—"

"No!" Claudio bellowed, cracking François's head against the wall again and again. "Don't you dare use my name!"

A look of abject desperation crossed François' face as he dropped his weapon and tried to pry loose Claudio's fingers. Blood trickled over his collar. Real fear shone in his eyes. "Please..."

Claudio threw him to the floor. François slid several yards, leaving a wide trail of blood. Before he had come to a stop, Claudio had picked up the dropped rapier and advanced on him. "Jean, bring my sword! Stand up!" he commanded François.

"No, Claude-Michel, don't do this. You'll see, when you calm down, you'll understand why I did it."

"Stand up or I will kill you where you lay."

François stood and took the sword Jean handed him, half-heartedly blocking the blows that Claudio dealt. Then he heaved a sigh and stood still. "Claude-Michel, I—"

But Claudio did not stop. He dealt a final blow, slicing right through François' wrist and causing his sword to clatter to the floor, still clutched by his right hand. A look of shock came over François' face as he stared at it, then at the blood spewing from his limb. Claudio backed away as droplets sprayed his face. François screamed and clutched the arm to him, cast an injured look at Claudio, and fled.

"If you ever return, I will kill you!" Claudio screamed after him.

Jean stood by the wall, his eyes widened in shock. I don't know what I did. I felt as though I had disappeared, and that the scene in front of my eyes was all that existed. "Tell Bernardo and Florentine to clean this up and get rid of that," Claudio said, nodding at François' severed hand.

Jean did not move, but continued to stare at the blood-covered corridor.

"Jean!" Claudio shouted.

The boy blinked and nodded, looking as though he may be sick. "*Oui, Monsieur.*"

"And see if we have something left for my daughter to eat."

"Florentine already did," Jean said. "There is some bread and wine. I can get more in the morning."

"We will get more tonight," Claudio said, wiping the blood from his face as he strode toward the stairs. "We are going to find a doctor and bring him here by force if necessary. And if you ever see François Villaforte again, tell me," he said, on the way down the stairs. I did not understand why he wasn't with his daughter.

"Claudio?" I called. "Where are you going?"

"To save my daughter's life."

I advanced on him, standing close and whispering too low for the girl to hear. "She wants you here. It is a miracle she has lived this long. If she dies tonight wanting to be with you, how will you feel?"

"A doctor can save her," he said.

"A doctor couldn't save the other woman, could he? Your daughter wants you to be with her tonight. She is frightened and she misses you. Will you leave her again when you have the chance to comfort her?"

He looked at Jean, who lowered his eyes, then turned back to me. Without speaking, he walked slowly back up the stairs. "Get me water and something to clean myself with," he said to Jean.

Jean nodded hastily and left. Claudio stood and stared at the blood in the hall, then bellowed in rage and threw his weapon.

I stayed with Claudio, who spent the night propped up in Camille's bed, letting her curl next to his leg, stroking her hair and back. She had managed to eat some of the bread and drink some of the wine Florentine had brought. Sometime during the night, Camille woke with a start, blinked at him and smiled. "I thought you were a dream," she said.

"No, *papillon*. I am no dream. Try to sleep."

For a few days it seemed as though she was getting better. She told us about François' insistence that Claudio was dead and his own promise to return, how Maurice and his wife had stayed and cared for them, how the sickness had come and Angelique had cared for Maurice's wife as she died. Claudio held her as she cried for her mother.

"She missed you so much," Camille said. "Every day she talked to your portrait. Each time she thought she had done something wrong, she told you. She would bow in front of that painting for hours." She turned her tear-damp face up to him. "Why did she do that, Papa? I thought I should do it too, but it made my knees hurt."

"It was her special way of showing her devotion to me," he said.

Bernardo came in with fresh water. I could see on Claudio's face that the boy's smell caused Claudio to feel his hunger. He had had no appetite for days, but now his hunger rose to the surface, too quickly to hide. His teeth grew quickly. Horrified, he turned his face from Camille, but she had already seen.

"Papa," she asked with a note of pure astonishment. "What has happened to your teeth?"

"Nothing," he said. "It is your fever."

"Do you want to get some fresh air, *Monsieur*?" I asked.

"Papa, let me see," Camille insisted. Her begging was filled with so much longing, he could do nothing but bow his head. "Please, Papa. Is this why you didn't come back? Are you a vampire?"

He turned back to her. "What? What do you know of vampires?"

"There are stories. People say they aren't true, but I always thought—Papa! Your teeth!"

His fangs had reached their full length. My heart raced on his behalf as I remembered the look of hatred on Lucio's face. He had been betrayed by one child already. Another such betrayal, I feared, might kill him. But Claudio, whatever else he is, is a strong man who does what he must, so he took a deep breath and turned to her. "Yes," he said carefully. "I am a vampire, as are Chloe and François. It is something that happened to us during our travels."

Camille's eyes widened. "Do you kill people and drink their blood?"

He chuckled wearily. "No," he said. "It doesn't happen in that way. They don't die. They stay with me so I can feed from them."

"Is that what Bernardo and Florentine do? Stay with you so you can eat?"

"Yes," he said. "And Jean, of course." He smiled sheepishly.

"Are you hungry now?" she asked.

He nodded.

"You should go drink. Then come back." She clutched his hand as she spoke, as if afraid he may disappear into the darkness again.

He lifted her hand to his lips. "My *papillon*. I will not leave you again."

She smiled and closed her eyes, dropping off to sleep immediately.

"She's been keeping herself awake to be with you," I said. "The rest will do her some good."

Claudio nodded and left, calling for Bernardo, while I kept watch over Camille. But things did not go well for her during that nap, and she was feverish when Claudio returned a half-hour later.

He stood by the bed, touching the sheet absently. "I didn't take her to the theatre," he said.

"The theatre?"

"She wanted me to take her for a walk in the park, as I had when she was younger, but I was too busy with Gabriel, her brother. Trying to find a wife for him. So I told her I would take her to the theatre Thursday evening. But by that time, I was gone."

I stood and went to him, surprised by the depth of his feeling for his family. It broke my heart. It is probably the reason I came to love him as I do. I took his hand in mine and kissed it. "She bears you no ill will, Claudio. She is very happy right now. Happy that you've come back."

"I left my wife to die alone."

"You didn't know. It was François. Not you. François is to blame for this."

He sat on the edge of Camille's bed, stroking her matted hair. "It hardly matters anymore where the blame falls."

Claudio had not moved when she came to later. Her voice was very weak. "Papa..."

He looked into her eyes and tried to smile. "I am here, *papillon*."

"Papa, I'm sick."

"You will be well soon," he said.

"Papa...if you bite me..."

"Shh....don't speak such nonsense."

"She's right, Claudio," I said, leaning toward him. "It could help her."

Camille began to cough, fighting for breath. Claudio looked around as though there were someone there who could help her, but there was no one else in the room besides us. Finally, Camille's coughing quieted and she took in a few greedy gulps of air. "If you bite me, will I get better?"

He and I looked at each other. For the first time since we had come here, I was filled with hope. "They do seem to get stronger," I said.

Claudio turned back to Camille. "Do you want me to try? It will hurt."

"I want to see what it's like," she said.

He took her in his arms, trying not to embrace her too tightly. "My *papillon*, my little one. I don't want to cause you pain."

"Please," she said weakly.

With trembling hands, he moved the strands of hair that clung to her throat. The strands would not cooperate with his trembling fingers, so I helped. There had been many terrifying nights in my past caring for sick children, and I knew how to set aside my fears to do small things, just as the soldier in Claudio knew how to set aside his fears to do big things. Camille smiled at him. "Like this?" she asked and leaned back her head, exposing her throat to him.

Claudio's eyes filled with tears. He closed them tight and kissed her flushed cheek. Then, with a resigned sigh, he moved his lips to her throat and used the tip of his tongue to find the spot. She tensed and gasped as he slid his fangs into her, clutching at him.

He shut his eyes tight and made a face as he drank. I knew the blood must be bitter. He drank only a little, and set her down. She smiled sleepily up at him. "Don't cry, Papa," she said.

He tried to smile at her, but a strange expression came over him. Then he was at the chamber pot, vomiting. By the time he had turned back, Camille was asleep. I went to him and put my arms around him.

* * * *

The following afternoon, Camille woke suddenly and demanded food and a favorite book, which she sat up reading most of the day. After a few hours of this, I was able to coax Claudio out for a walk.

"I am going to take her away from here," he said. "We have to leave this house as soon as she is strong enough." We found ourselves at a cluster of three graves—his son Gabriel's, Angelique's and Claudio's own. "It is odd to gaze at one's own grave," he said. "So much of me has died."

"I am sorry, *Monsieur*, about this. And about François," I said.

Claudio swallowed. "We have been together since we were very young boys. And I never knew he would...destroy everything."

"He is mad with desire for you," I said quietly.

"To think my Angelique suffered here alone," he said. "I would kill him. But I know that banishment is a far worse punishment than death."

We returned to Camille's room to find Victoire looking after her. She brightened when she saw Claudio. "Papa," she said. "I feel better."

"That is wonderful," he said. For the first time since I had known him, he looked genuinely happy.

"Uncle Victoire was reading to me."

Victoire stood up. "And now it is time to go in search of wine and bread, since I am cursed to remain as I am," he said, smiling sweetly at me before leaving the room.

"What is that about?" Claudio asked.

"He wants to be a vampire," I told him. "He asked me to do it before we came to Paris."

"I think you should," Camille said. "Two brothers. Two vampires. It's romantic."

"You have an odd notion of romance," Claudio said. "But soon you will be able to travel, and fill your head with foreign lands," he said.

"Where are we going?"

"To find the most beautiful park in the world, so that I can show off the most beautiful girl in the world and make all of the young men jealous." He bent down and kissed the top of her head.

"The park...and the theatre?"

"But of course," he said. "Especially the theatre."

He stayed with her the rest of the afternoon. When I left him to find my own meal, he was telling her of his adventures, and of Gunnar and Lucio. And Katarina.

But late that night she became worse, crying out with delusions. He called for Jean. "Go find a doctor. Bring him back on the tip of your sword if you must, but bring him back!"

Claudio held Camille's trembling body close as she cried and mumbled incoherent words. Before long, however, she went limp in his arms. I could do nothing for him as he held his dying child in his arms. Jean returned many hours later, alone.

"He would not come, Monsieur. And when I drew my sword, he laughed at me and threw me out. I could not find another. Monsieur, what is wrong?"

"It is no matter," Claudio said dully. "I doubt he could have done anything."

The men buried her next to her brother. We stayed one more day in the house. Claudio wandered from room to room like a ghost. It was late afternoon the next day when we left. On the main road, there were three young men walking. "Stop the carriage," Claudio said. "Stop the carriage!"

The young men, full of drink, laughed. "What does the respectable gentleman want?" one of them called.

"Are you familiar with le Chateau du Fresne?" he asked.

"Of course we are. We don't have money, but we know where it is."

Claudio tossed a pouch at them. It landed at the speaker's feet. One of the other two scrambled to pick it up and reach inside. "It is mine," Claudio said. "I want you to burn it. Burn everything. Keep nothing. Do you understand?"

The young man counting the money whispered to the speaker, who nodded, his tone changed to disbelief. "*Oui, Monsieur.* We will."

"Very good," he said. "Jean. Drive."

Chapter 20

CLAUDIO HAD Jean drive us to the apartment where he took his mistresses and lovers, and then had him get the spare key hidden under a stone in a nearby garden. "It is amazing that it hasn't been stolen away from me, yes?" he said. Behind us, a passing older gentleman cleared his throat. Claudio turned and gave him a stiff smile.

The old man looked with interest from one of us to another—Victoire, his Pierre, Jean, Bernardo, Florentine and myself—before returning to Claudio with a look approaching admiration.

"Yes?" Claudio said with a hint of impatience.

"*Perdone, Monsieur*, but I heard news that le Compte du Fresne had gone away, yet you look remarkably like him. And this is, if I am not mistaken, his apartment."

"Don't be ridiculous," Claudio said. "I've met the man. He is much shorter."

He opened the door and stepped inside the stale, dusty parlor just as the gentleman wished him a happy evening, albeit with a look of longing that suggested he would like nothing more than to be invited inside. As soon as we stepped over the threshold, though, Claudio quickly shut the door. Jean went into the bedroom with our things.

The parlor was furnished with a bar, a reading chair, and a bookshelf on which Claudio kept many of the erotic works of the day. Florentine seemed drawn to them, making a little "Oh!" sound and putting a hand up to her mouth with a giggle upon reading a few of the titles. Excitedly, she pulled one out. Bernardo came over.

"Florentine!" he admonished. "You mustn't read such things." When he attempted to take it, she clutched the book to her breast and turned away.

"Leave me alone, Bernardo."

"But Florentine..."

I felt amused as I listened. Bernardo sometimes clung so tightly to his old life, even though he was becoming adept at servicing vampires. I drifted to the window just as Florentine rounded on her brother and brandished the book at him. "You would have sent me into a marriage knowing nothing, and you expect me to remain ignorant even now. Remain the object of a man's desire while taking no thought for my own pleasure?"

"It isn't respectable for a young lady—"

"If being respectable means being dead inside, Bernardo, then I don't want to be respectable!" She plopped into Claudio's reading chair, gave Bernardo a parting glare, and opened the book, breathing heavily. Bernardo opened his mouth to continue, but Claudio stopped him.

"Let her read," he said. "I for one wouldn't mind if she learned something. And if you keep bothering her, she may injure you."

Victoire joined me on the balcony. "I was serious," he said. "I have given it thought. I want to become as you are.

I would appreciate it if you would consider doing this for me."

I nodded. "Has Claude-Michel said anything to you about it? I told him."

He shook his head. "He has had things on his mind. But now, perhaps he will be free to think of something other than revenge."

"Perhaps. I will consider your request, Victoire, but I think you should speak with your brother. I won't do it if he says no."

"Fair enough."

"And I don't know how long it will be before I can do it again, at any rate."

Behind us, Bernardo stormed into the bedroom. I left the balcony to Victoire and sat with Florentine, who was only pretending to read. She pressed her lips together angrily and breathed heavily. I tried to take her mind off of her brother. "Will you read it to me sometime?" I asked.

"Read it to you? Wouldn't you rather read it your—" She narrowed her eyes, studying me closely. "You don't know how to read?" she asked, astonished.

I felt embarrassed, which was a thing that did not happen often. "I did not grow up as you did."

"But you seem to know so much..."

"There are different ways of learning," I said.

"Come here," Florentine said. "I can teach you..."

And so it was the day after the last of le Compte Claude-Michel du Fresne's life had died. Claudio wandered around the place, touching his things. I wondered if he felt he was touching things that had belonged to someone else, and if he was imagining happy afternoons spent here in the arms of beautiful young men and women. I wondered, also, if he had the same sense I did, that finally we were starting our new lives. I, for one, had never imagined my life would change so drastically. I was going to go to him as he threw open the windows and gazed out on the streets below, but Jean came back into the room and stood by him instead.

"Bernardo has claimed the couch in the bedroom," he said. "He says he refuses to sleep in a bed of decadence."

Florentine snorted softly but did not look up from her book.

"He will learn," Claudio said. "Perhaps he will appreciate the company of a young man near his age. Perhaps you can help him understand pleasure."

Jean nodded. "What are we going to do, Monsieur?"

"Whatever we want," Claudio said. "There is always the New World. Perhaps it will benefit from a civilizing influence. But for now," he said, "I want you to buy food and wine. I put some money in your pouch."

When Jean had gone, Claudio went into the bedroom. Florentine and I looked at each other. A wicked smile began to form on her lips. "Let's go," I said. We found Claudio with his violin, and all thoughts of mischief left us. He had not touched it since I had brought it home, and I had wondered if he liked it at all. But now, he handled it with such gentleness. At the first touch of the bow, it screeched as if in pain, but he adjusted it patiently. First one string, then another, then back to the first, until the sounds it made were something approaching music. Then he put it aside and stood, smiling wickedly at me and Florentine, just before turning to Bernardo, who closed his eyes just as Claudio turned toward him. A normal man, I thought, would not have seen the boy's eyelids move, but I knew Claudio had, as I had. Claudio smiled just a little, then began to remove his blouse. When he was nude, he lay down. Florentine and I joined him.

While I undressed on the other side of the bed, Florentine perched on her knees between us and kissed him on the lips. "Have you decided I am not a monster?" he teased.

"You have done nothing to me a husband would not have," she said with a shrug. "And that was a life to which I had resigned myself." She tilted her head and grinned. "But you are much more handsome, and I am glad that other man is gone."

Claudio scowled. "François?"

My heart lurched at the mere sound of his name. I wondered when we would see him again. Gunnar used to tell me that exiled vampires always had a habit of returning. They lived so long, it was inevitable.

Florentine nodded. "I did not like him."

"Well," Claudio said, pulling her close. "You will not have to worry about him again." Nude, I climbed on top of him, straddling his hips with my thighs. He looked up at me. "You look very pleased with yourself," he said.

"We have reached an agreement," I said. "She will teach me to read, and I will teach her other things."

She and I shared a look, then a kiss.

"Ah," Claudio said. "Poor, poor Jean. We will be exhausted by the time he returns," he said, and began untying Florentine's bodice.

* * * *

Florentine and I began to stir late in the afternoon, and found ourselves in the bed alone. Bernardo lay on the couch with his back to us and his arms crossed. Jean poured wine for us as we stumbled into the parlor, awakened by the first hesitant sounds of Claudio's violin.

"Oooh," Florentine said, accepting her glass. "Play something lively." She yawned. We were all still nude from our afternoon tryst. Jean had taken off his shoes and let his hair down, and Bernardo would not come out of the bedroom.

"Lively," Claudio said, thinking. "This one." He launched into an old dance tune he had heard Katarina's father play long ago. "I am surprised my fingers can find this one," he said. I watched him and, for a moment, saw him as I had the very first time. He smiled as he played.

Florentine opened her mouth wide and laughed, then sprang into the middle of the floor and grabbed Jean's hand, making him dance. Then she let him go and came to me, tugging me toward Jean, dancing with both of us. When the tune ended she clapped her hands in childlike glee.

"That was wonderful!" she said. "Play another."

Claudio glanced toward the bedroom door. "Bernardo should be with us. It is not good for him to sulk so much."

Florentine pouted. "I would prefer it if he stayed away," she said loudly.

Claudio clicked his tongue. "I see I will be forced to spank the two of you like children," he said. "Jean, tell Bernardo we will dress if he is bothered by such a display of bodies. But make it clear I expect him to come here and stop acting like a spoiled child."

"*Oui, Monsieur*," Jean said, and went into the bedroom. The next moment, Bernardo appeared in the doorway like a ruffled cherub.

"I apologize, *Monsieur*," he said, glancing at his sister, then turning his head. "This is all so strange."

Claudio approached him, his hair wild from sleeping and sex and playing. "This is pleasure. In return for taking your body—and your sister—I will provide for you pleasure and freedom. Adventures. Every young man dreams of adventures, no? I know the life you've left behind, Bernardo. It can be a prison. But you and I, we are free men."

He nodded. "I will try, since it seems I have no choice."

"Good boy. Jean, wine for Bernardo," he said with a flourish of his free hand. "Chloe, dance with him. Florentine is a terrible slave-mistress who wants me to play until I drop of exhaustion," he said, flashing her a wicked smile. She returned it, then trotted off to the bedroom.

"I will put on clothes for my dear, dear brother," she said in the voice of a taunting child.

"I will join her," I said.

Jean drank his wine as though kissing it from the glass, keeping his eyes on Bernardo, laughing at his discomfort. When we returned in our nightgowns, Bernardo came to me as though for protection. Claudio smiled, and continued to play. I think we were innocent in some way then, because we were so young.

As the afternoon light faded, Claudio played, still nude, telling stories of ageless Pan and his pipes. He did not stop until twilight made the sky purple, and we stopped dancing to stare out the window with gasps, and cries of, "Look!" Then, the tune he had been playing screeched to a halt and he walked to the window.

"My house," he said.

In the distance, a fire raged, and we knew the young men he paid had kept their word.

"You will have a new house," I whispered. He nodded. I could feel his body shift suddenly, as though something swelled inside him. Again, he brought the violin to his chin and he began to play. Somehow, I knew it was different—not as he had played tonight and not as he had played for the women he had seduced long ago. Tonight, there was fire, and music that poured from his body like blood to silence his family with its beauty, as primal and haunting as the crashing of the sea.

The End

Also Available from Red Silk Editions

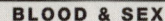

Blood & Sex: Michael
by Angela Cameron

This is a spine-chilling and erotic tale of a Mafia vampire and the detective who is determined to bring to justice a serial killer. Detective Victoria Tyler allows Mafia vampire Michael to "take her neck" and lead her on a journey through a world of bondage, domination, and blood to stop the killer. But can she resist the dark lusts he sparks?

Volume 1 in the Blood & Sex series

Paperback: $12.95

978-1-59003-203-9

Available in August 2010

Blood & Sex: Jonas
by Angela Cameron

Jonas, the strangely appealing owner of the new vampire-themed bondage club could be the perfect distraction for workaholic Dr. Elena Jensen. But their worlds couldn't be farther apart....

Volume 2 of the Blood & Sex series

Paperback: $12.95

978-1-59003-202-2

Available in October 2010

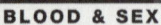

Blood & Sex: Blane
by Angela Cameron

Will Blane be able to break through the guarded reserve of Christiana, the beautiful woman the vampire leader has sent to educate the newest vampires? Or will her sense of duty be stronger than the passion that threatens to sweep her away?

Volume 3 of the Blood & Sex series

Paperback: $12.95

978-1-59003-206-0

Available in December 2010

The Maestro's Butterfly
by Rhonda Leigh Jones

Miranda O'Connell has just made a dangerous bet with her mysterious, sexy music teacher that will change her life forever. Will she fall in love with the kinky vampire Maestro and submit to life as a feeder slave? Or will she escape the confines of his estate for the dashing, dangerous charms of his brother?

Paperback: $12.95

978-1-59003-207-7

Available in November 2010

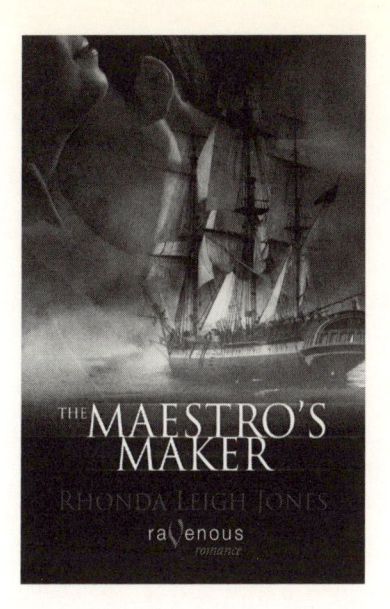

The Maestro's Maker
by Rhonda Leigh Jones

Trapped between two vampires: Chloe discovers the darkness that binds the beautiful and arrogant French noble Claudio du Fresne and his oldest friend Francois Villaforte. With danger, intrigue, and kinky sex, *The Maestro's Maker* takes vampire erotica to passionate new levels!

Paperback: $12.95

978-1-59003-210-7

Available in December 2010

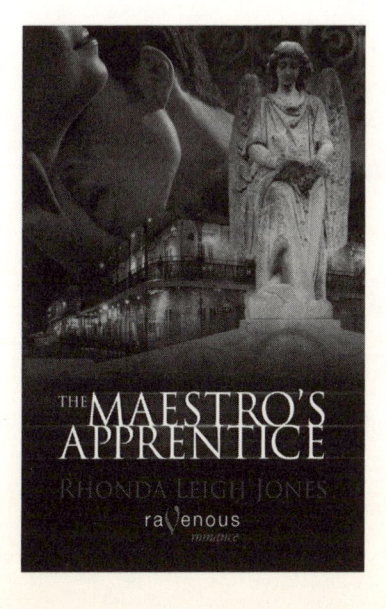

The Maestro's Apprentice
by Rhonda Leigh Jones

For the first time in her life, Autumn is free. She has escaped Claudio du Fresne, the vampire for whom she had been a feeder-slave for years. Now she wants to play, and for her, playing means wild, crazy sex with strangers.

Paperback: $12.95

978-1-59003-209-1

Available in January 2011

The Dark Desires of the Druids: Sex & Subterfuge
by Isabel Roman

"Do you like jealous heroes and love triangles? How about sizzling sexual encounters atop dining room furniture? If you answered yes to either question, you're going to love this novella."
—Susan S., loveromance.passion.com

Paperback: $12.95

978-1-59003-200-8

Available in August 2010

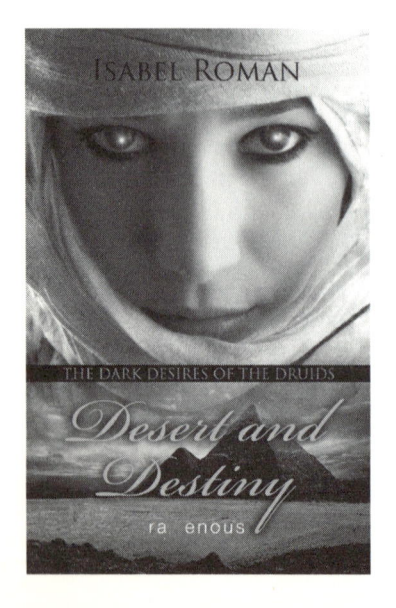

The Dark Desires of the Druids: Desert and Destiny
by Isabel Roman

The first time they met, Arbelle Bahari tried to kill him. The second time, they made love on a desk in the British Museum.

"The action is fast and exciting, the mystery is engaging, and the romance is searingly hot." —*Whipped Cream Reviews* (5 Cherries)

Paperback: $12.95

978-1-59003-201-5

Available in October 2010

Bites of Passion
edited by Cecilia Tan

What does it mean to love a vampire? Does it mean nights of pleasure tempered with sweet pain? Eight top authors explore the themes of immortal love, the lust for blood, and the eternal struggle between light and dark.

Paperback: $12.95

978-1-59003-205-3

Available in September 2010

Magic University: The Siren and the Sword
by Cecilia Tan

Harvard freshman Kyle Wadsorth is eager to start a new life. Surprises abound when he discovers a secret magical university hidden inside Harvard and he meets Jess Torralva, who tutors him in the ways of magic, sex, and love.

Paperback: $12.95

978-1-59003-208-4

Available in November 2010

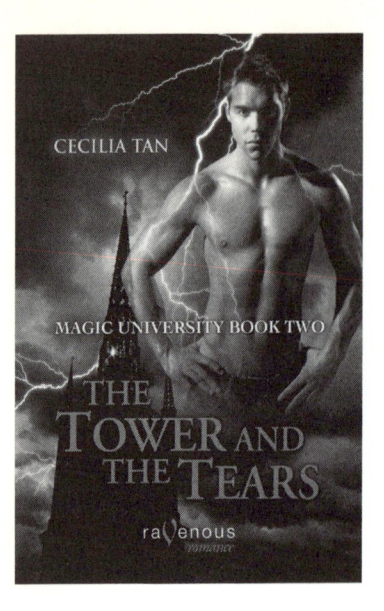

Magic University: The Tower and the Tears by Cecilia Tan

This second volume in the Magic University series brings together myth, magic, and eroticism for adult readers of fantasy who want a bedtime tale of their own.

"Simply one of the most important writers, editors, and innovators in contemporary American erotic literature." —Susie Bright

Paperback: $12.95

978-1-59003-211-4

Available in January 2011

Mind Games
by Cecilia Tan

Who hasn't fantasized about using psychic abilities to satisfy your every sexual desire? *Mind Games* provides readers the opportunity to live out that dream....

"Scorching hot with a touch of suspense. Cecilia Tan brings together love, suspense, and scorching sex in a story well worth reading." —*ParaNormal Romance Review*

Paperback: $12.95

978-1-59003-204-6

Available in September 2010